Elizabeth Knows Best

Jessica looked at Elizabeth carefully. "People are saying Todd would make a pretty good candidate for Model Student."

Elizabeth finished folding a pillowcase. "Todd?" she repeated.

"He's got all the characteristics of a Model Student, don't you think?" Jessica continued. "I mean, he gets good grades, he's involved in a lot of different activities, and everybody respects him."

Elizabeth frowned and put her hands on her hips. "Whose side are you on, Jessica? It just so happens that I don't agree that Todd Wilkins would be as good a candidate as I am. And it also happens that I'm right more often than you are."

Jessica stared open-mouthed at her twin. This was an Elizabeth she had never seen before.

"Well, I am," Elizabeth insisted, as if Jessica had contradicted her.

Jessica felt herself beginning to get angry. "I just think you should consider the possibility—"

"You have to admit, Jessica, that your bright ideas are usually dim-witted," Elizabeth interrupted.

This time, Jessica couldn't control herself. "Elizabeth," she shouted, "you are being a total jerk!"

Bantam Skylark Books in the SWEET VALLEY TWINS series
Ask your bookseller for the books you have missed

SWEET VALLEY TWINS

Elizabeth
the
Impossible

◇

Written by
Jamie Suzanne

Created by
FRANCINE PASCAL

A BANTAM SKYLARK BOOK
NEW YORK · TORONTO · LONDON · SYDNEY · AUCKLAND

RL 4, 008–012

ELIZABETH THE IMPOSSIBLE
A Bantam Skylark Book / August 1991

Elizabeth
the
Impossible

One

◇

"I just *love* your new outfit, Elizabeth," Pamela McDonald gushed Friday at lunch. "That blue-green color matches your eyes perfectly."

"Thanks, Pamela," Elizabeth Wakefield answered. She and Pamela sat down at the lunch table across from Amy Sutton, Julie Porter, and Sophia Rizzo. For several weeks, Pamela had been following Elizabeth around, treating her as if she were the most extraordinary thing that ever hit Sweet Valley. Pamela had even gone so far as to copy the way Elizabeth dressed and wore her hair! It was getting to be more than a little embarrassing.

Amy looked up from her Swiss cheese sandwich. "It's new, isn't it?" she asked. "Your outfit, I mean."

"I bought it with some of the money I got for writing the column in the *Tribune*," Elizabeth replied, opening her carton of milk. The *Tribune*, Sweet Valley's local newspaper, had recently run a series of special columns called "The Junior Journalist." The columns were written by carefully selected students from different schools and featured stories about kids who were helping other people. To Elizabeth's surprise, she had been named as the Junior Journalist from Sweet Valley Middle School.

"I think you wrote a terrific column, Elizabeth," Pamela said, her round face glowing with admiration. "When I read it, I just knew I *had* to get to know you better. *I've* always wanted to be a writer, too." She paused and ran her fingers through her dark hair. "But I know I'll never be as good as you are. *Nobody* could be that good!"

Elizabeth cringed at Pamela's last remark. She could see Amy snickering behind her sandwich, and even Sophia was grinning.

Julie ignored Pamela's compliment. "I still can't believe you earned fifty dollars and a byline by writing a story about the Unicorns doing a good deed," she said.

Amy laughed. "Yeah. Who would have believed that the Unicorns could ever do anything for anybody but themselves?"

Elizabeth had to laugh, too. Her story had featured the Skate-a-Thon that the exclusive Unicorn Club had sponsored to raise money for a new encyclopedia for the school library. The Unicorn Club consisted of the prettiest and most popular girls at Sweet Valley Middle School. Usually, the only thing the Unicorns raised money for was their own parties.

The buzz of conversation hushed as the assistant principal stepped up onto the platform at the front of the cafeteria. "I have a special announcement to make," Mr. Edwards said. "Just this morning I received an unexpected phone call from an editor at *Teen Scene* magazine." Mr. Edwards paused. "It seems that one of our very own students recently entered their nationwide essay contest."

"Hey, Elizabeth," Amy whispered, "is that the essay contest you entered?"

Elizabeth nodded. Her essay was titled "Becoming an Individual," and it focused on the challenge of being both a twin *and* an individual. In her article, she described how she and her sister, Jessica, were identical twins. They both had long blond hair, blue-green eyes, and a dimple in their left cheeks. For many years, they had dressed alike and worn their hair alike. Not many people outside their family could tell the twins apart. But as they grew older, the twins realized how different they really were, and how important it was for each twin to have her own identity.

Elizabeth was the more serious and responsible twin. She loved reading her favorite Amanda Howard mysteries, writing for the class newspaper, *The Sweet Valley Sixers*, and spending time with her best friend, Amy Sutton.

Jessica, on the other hand, preferred to spend as much time as possible with her fellow members of the Unicorn Club, talking about boys, trying out new makeup, and going shopping at the mall. Jessica loved excitement—things like schoolwork and chores were much too dull for her. "Twins are special," Elizabeth had written in the essay, "but each *person* is special, too. I like being a twin, and I *love* being myself."

Mr. Edwards cleared his throat and continued

his announcement. "I am proud to say that the prize-winning essay, chosen from thousands of entries, was written by none other than our very own *Elizabeth Wakefield*!"

A loud cheer filled the cafeteria. "Way to go, Elizabeth," Winston Egbert called out.

Amy ran around the table to hug Elizabeth. "Congratulations!" she said excitedly.

"Elizabeth!" Sophia exclaimed. "That's terrific!"

"It's quite an honor, Elizabeth," Julie agreed.

"I can't believe it," Elizabeth said, shaking her head. She had thought her essay was good, but not good enough to be chosen over all the other essays, written by kids from all over the country.

"The prize," Mr. Edwards continued, "is a check for two hundred dollars and an all-expense-paid trip for two to Los Angeles to visit the magazine's headquarters. Elizabeth and her guest will tour the *Teen Scene* offices and meet the staff. Her essay will also be featured in an upcoming issue of the magazine."

"Two hundred dollars!" Amy's eyes were wide. "Awe-*some*!"

"And a trip to Los Angeles!" Julie added.

Pamela sighed and clasped her hands. "Elizabeth, you are absolutely, without exception, the most talented person in the entire world."

Elizabeth blushed. She knew that Amy and the others were just as fed up with Pamela's excessive compliments as she was. How would she ever get her to stop?

Elizabeth was relieved when Pamela stood and picked up her lunch tray. "I have to go, Elizabeth," Pamela said. "Why don't I wait for you after school and walk you home?"

"Elizabeth's coming to *my* house," Amy cut in quickly.

"I'll call you tomorrow, then, Elizabeth," Pamela said, ignoring Amy. "Maybe we can get together over the weekend."

Amy rolled her eyes as Pamela walked away. "I've never encountered anyone like Pamela McDonald before. She's totally bananas over you!"

"I know," Elizabeth said ruefully. "I wish I could get her to stop. Now I know what Maria Slater must have felt like all those years!" Maria Slater had recently moved to Sweet Valley from Los Angeles. She had been a child star, but now her career was temporarily over. Even harder, she had told Elizabeth, than realizing she was a has-been at the age of twelve, was handling unwelcome attention from fawning fans.

Sophia laughed. "A few compliments never hurt anyone, Elizabeth. And winning a national essay contest *is* pretty impressive!"

Amy groaned. "Come on, Sophia. Not you, too!"

All four girls were laughing when Todd Wilkins joined them. Todd was Elizabeth's boyfriend.

"Congratulations, Elizabeth!" Todd said, grinning. "You're the greatest!"

"No, Todd!" Amy pleaded, with mock-seriousness. "Don't tell her that!"

"But it's true, Amy," Todd protested. "How many other kids do you know who win national essay contests?"

"And who deserves to win as much as Elizabeth?" Sophia added. "Who has as many friends and admirers and—"

Amy winked at Elizabeth. "OK, OK! But you'd better not let all this fame go to your head, Elizabeth."

Elizabeth grinned. It was terrific to have won all that money and the trip and also to have been recognized for her writing. But the best prize of all was having friends who liked her for who she was, not what she did. Nothing she won could be worth more than that!

Jessica Wakefield had skipped lunch on Friday afternoon to help the Unicorns put up some posters announcing that the new encyclopedia had just arrived in the library. She did not know that Elizabeth had won the *Teen Scene* essay contest until Caroline Pearce caught up with her in front of the library.

"Have you heard the news?" Caroline asked importantly. Caroline wrote a gossip column for the *Sixers,* and she prided herself on knowing all the gossip first. "Elizabeth won first prize in the *Teen Scene* essay contest."

"*First* prize?" Jessica cried. "Terrific!"

"What did she win?" Mandy Miller asked.

"Two hundred dollars and a trip for two to the magazine's office in Los Angeles," Caroline said.

"I'll bet she'll get to stay in the very best hotel," Ellen Riteman said enviously.

"What a lucky break for Elizabeth," Lila Fower remarked.

Jessica gave Lila a scornful look. "Luck had

nothing to do with it. Elizabeth is an exceptionally talented writer."

"She must be," Mandy agreed. "She's won a total of two hundred and fifty dollars so far. You don't get that by being lucky."

"Maybe Elizabeth will loan you some of her prize money, Jessica," Lila suggested. "You could buy that fabulous purple belt with the matching tights we saw yesterday." She smiled. "After all, you *are* twins. Share and share alike, you know."

"Or maybe you could take her shopping and help her pick out some more exciting clothes," Ellen said. "Somebody who wins a national prize should *look* like a prize-winner."

Jessica shook her head. "I'm not telling Elizabeth how to spend her prize money," she said firmly. "I'm glad she won it, and I'm really proud of her."

"You have a right to be proud, Jessica," Mandy said. "It's not everybody who has a sister like Elizabeth."

"Mandy's right, Jessica," Ellen said thoughtfully. "I'm not exactly a fan of Elizabeth's, but I have to admit, she deserves to win the contest. I really liked her story about us in the *Tribune*. She mentioned *my* name at least three times."

Jessica nodded. "The best thing about Elizabeth is that no matter how many honors she gets, she's modest about it."

"That's my girl," Mr. Wakefield said as he gave Elizabeth a hug later that evening. "You've got great talent."

"We are *very* proud of you," Mrs. Wakefield added warmly. "Just think—out of thousands of essays from all over the country, yours was considered the best!"

Jessica nodded. "Everybody at school is talking about Elizabeth."

"A trip to Los Angeles, huh?" Steven, the twins' fourteen-year-old brother said. He grinned. "Yeah, Shrimp, you did OK."

Mr. Wakefield glanced at Mrs. Wakefield. "Don't you think this calls for a celebration dinner?"

Mrs. Wakefield smiled and nodded. "And Elizabeth gets to choose the restaurant."

"How about Guido's Pizza Palace?" Elizabeth suggested.

"Great idea, Elizabeth," Jessica confirmed. "I'll have pepperoni *and* anchovies on my pizza."

"And lots of cheese on mine," Steven said.

"Well, then, let's go." Mr. Wakefield gave Elizabeth one more hug. "We don't want to keep our famous author hungry!"

Two

◇

Jessica had just settled into her seat in homeroom on Monday morning when Mr. Davis passed out a small blue booklet. The question "Are *You* a Model Student?" was printed in big red letters across the cover.

When Jerry McAlister got his booklet, he snickered loudly and leaned across the aisle to Charlie Cashman. "Hey, Charlie," he said, "am *I* a model student?"

Jessica laughed. Jerry was about as far from being a model student as she could imagine.

Mr. Davis looked sternly at Jerry. "Would you like to discuss that question with me after school, Jerry?" he asked, and this time everybody laughed.

Mr. Davis held up the booklet. "This booklet announces a nationwide search for the best middle-grade students in the country," he said. "Depending on its size, every middle school gets to nominate at least one candidate."

Caroline Pearce raised her hand. "What do you have to do to be a model student, Mr. Davis?" she asked, flipping her red hair over her shoulders.

"The answer to your question is on page four of the booklet, Caroline," Mr. Davis replied.

Jessica turned to page four. At the top of the page were the words *The Model Student Guide*, and underneath them were listed all the attributes of a Model Student. According to the list, a Model Student got good grades, was respected by teachers and fellow students, and was conscientious, friendly, cheerful, and trustworthy. And that was just the beginning.

Behind Jessica, Ellen leaned forward. "Are *you* a Model Student, Jessica?" she whispered.

"I don't know," Jessica said. "I haven't finished the list yet." She read on. A Model Student had a sense of humor and assisted teachers. He or she participated in the creative and/or performing arts or in sports. A Model Student was well organized, neat, and healthy.

The bell rang, and Jessica slipped the booklet into her notebook. "I guess I'm not a Model Student," she told Ellen as they walked toward the door. "I'd have to get organized and give up candy and soda. I'd probably have to get more exercise, too. Too much work!"

Lila and Mandy joined Jessica and Ellen as they left the room. "You'd have to be a saint to win this stupid contest," Ellen said, sounding disgusted. "*Nobody* at Sweet Valley Middle School is that perfect."

"Nobody in the *world* is that perfect," Lila replied with a sniff.

"Elizabeth!" Jessica clapped her hands together suddenly.

"Elizabeth what?" Ellen asked.

"I'm going to nominate Elizabeth for Model Student," Jessica said excitedly. "She's perfect. In fact, she's *so* perfect that she gives *me* an inferiority complex."

Her friends laughed, but Jessica was serious. Sometimes it did bother her when people reminded her that her twin was neater, more responsible, and more dependable than she was. But right now, she wasn't complaining. Jessica was truly proud to have a sister like Elizabeth.

Mandy frowned. "Wait a minute," she said. "Didn't you read the booklet?"

"Not all of it," Jessica admitted. "Why?"

"Because kids don't nominate the Model Student," Mandy pointed out. "The teachers and the principal do it."

"Oh," Jessica replied. Then she lifted her chin. "Well, I guess that means I'll just have to make *sure* that the teachers and Mr. Clark nominate her."

Lila laughed. "That might not be so easy, Jessica. They probably have other kids in mind, too."

"I thought you said nobody in the world is that perfect," Jessica snapped. "How many Model Students can there be in one school?"

"Not *that* many," Lila acknowledged. "But there's bound to be one or two besides Elizabeth. And I'm sure the teachers know who they are."

"That's why I have to get busy," Jessica said, her eyes gleaming.

Mandy frowned. "You'd better not let Elizabeth know what you're up to," she cautioned. "I have a feeling she wouldn't like it if she knew you were trying to get the teachers to nominate her.''

Jessica nodded. "That's exactly why you guys aren't going to breathe a word of this to her—or to anybody else!''

During English class, Jessica tuned out Mr. Bowman's lecture on how to organize an essay and concentrated instead on how to organize her "Elizabeth for Model Student" campaign. Jessica finally decided that the best thing to do would be to talk to every teacher individually. After class, she marched up to Mr. Bowman's desk and waited while he repeated the assignment to Leslie Forsythe. When he had finished, Leslie smiled shyly at Jessica and scurried away.

"Did you miss the assignment, too, Jessica?'' Mr. Bowman asked with a frown.

Jessica *had* missed it, but she didn't want to admit that to Mr. Bowman. Anyway, she could get it from Elizabeth, who *never* missed an assignment. "I wanted to talk to you about the Model Student competition,'' she said.

Mr. Bowman's eyebrows shot up. "Are you suggesting that *you'd* be a good candidate, Jessica?'' he asked.

"No, not me," Jessica said hastily. "But I think Elizabeth would. The Model Student Guide sounds as if it were written about her."

Mr. Bowman seemed to be considering Jessica's statement. When he spoke, his tone was serious. "Well, you're right about that. I certainly was impressed with Elizabeth's winning the *Teen Scene* essay contest."

Jessica nodded happily. Mr. Bowman was playing right into her hands. "I was thinking about that, too," she said. "I wondered if maybe it could be reprinted in the *Sixers*, so everybody could read it. Elizabeth is far too modest to suggest printing it."

"That's a great idea," Mr. Bowman agreed. "As for the Model Student nomination, I'll give it some thought. Now, you'd better hurry, or you'll be late for your next class."

Jessica raced off. She was thrilled. When Elizabeth's essay was reprinted in the *Sixers*, all her teachers would read it and realize that Elizabeth was the best possible candidate for Model Student. Her scheme was working—and it had been so easy!

The next step—talking to Ms. Langberg, the gym teacher—was just as easy. Jessica went to the gym and pretended that she had left a pair of sneakers there after the last Boosters practice. After she conducted a phony search, she stood on the sidelines watching Elizabeth and Brooke Dennis practice a tumbling routine.

Jessica sighed loudly. "I wish I were as good as Elizabeth," she said as her twin snapped a back flip off the mat.

Ms. Langberg looked at Jessica. "Jessica, you *are* that good! You just need to put in a little more practice."

"That's it," Jessica agreed. "Elizabeth is good *and* she's dedicated. She's willing to practice for as long as it takes to get it right."

"Elizabeth certainly does stick to it," Ms. Langberg agreed.

"Then you've probably been thinking of her as a candidate for the Model Student competition," Jessica said smoothly. "I just talked to Mr. Bowman, and he said *he* was thinking about it."

Ms. Langberg raised her eyebrows. "Really? That's very interesting," she replied. She picked up her whistle. "You'd better get going, Jessica. You'll be late for whatever it is you *should* be doing now."

After her next class, Jessica checked to be sure

Elizabeth had left the room before she reminded Mrs. Arnette what a great job Elizabeth had done on a social studies project. "You're right, Jessica," Mrs. Arnette agreed.

"Well?" Lila asked as Jessica sat down at the Unicorner, the Unicorns favorite table, at lunchtime. "Have you gotten Elizabeth nominated yet?"

"Not yet," Jessica said. "But I will."

Ellen put some catsup on her hot dog. "I hope Elizabeth is grateful for everything you're doing for her," she said.

"If she weren't so modest," Jessica said, "she'd probably be campaigning for herself. I'll bet that's what other kids are doing—campaigning for themselves."

"You're right about that," Lila said with a laugh. "Caroline told me that Bruce Patman told Mr. Clark that *he* should be nominated."

Jessica laughed. All the Unicorns agreed that Bruce was the cutest boy in the seventh grade, but he was also the most conceited. She did not see *how* the teachers would nominate him over Elizabeth.

"Speaking of Bruce," Ellen whispered, "here he comes."

Jessica looked up to see Bruce Patman sauntering over to their table.

"Hey, guess what?" Bruce said. "Coach Cassels is thinking about nominating me for Model Student."

"Really?" Ellen asked.

"Yeah, really." Bruce grinned confidently. "Who else do you know who's superpopular, a good basketball player, *and* a natural-born leader?"

"Maybe you ought to add *conceited* to that list," Lila scoffed.

Bruce shrugged. "If you've got what it takes, why try to hide it?" he asked, and walked away.

Jessica frowned. If Coach Cassels was really thinking about nominating Bruce, she would have to take him seriously as competition for Elizabeth. And she could not trust Bruce. For all Jessica knew, he might have something up his sleeve. Now she would have to make an extra effort for her sister!

After history class, Jessica made a point of telling Mr. Nydick that Elizabeth had just finished coloring and lettering an entire book of maps. Mr. Nydick loved maps and was always showing them to the class. "I'll ask her to bring the book to class so I can show it to the others," he said.

"Elizabeth is *such* a good student," Jessica added pointedly. "She's a *model* for the rest of us." Mr. Nydick didn't look up from the papers he had begun to grade. "A real *model*," she continued.

This time Mr. Nydick glanced up and smiled. "She is indeed." Jessica left the room with the feeling that he'd gotten her message loud and clear.

In math class, Jessica told Ms. Wyler that Elizabeth had helped her to understand percentages. "Isn't that a trademark of a Model Student?" she asked. "I mean, being able to help other people understand their work?"

Ms. Wyler looked amused by Jessica's comment. "I'm glad to know that Elizabeth was helpful, Jessica," she said. "Perhaps she wouldn't mind tutoring some of the other students."

On the way to her locker after her last class, Jessica ran into Mr. Edwards, the assistant principal.

"Oh, hi, Mr. Edwards," Jessica said. "I wanted to thank you for making that announcement on Friday. About Elizabeth winning the essay contest, I mean."

Mr. Edwards looked surprised. "You don't have to thank me for something like that, Jessica. It's part of my job."

"Well, thanks just the same." Jessica smiled. "It's so wonderful to have a sister like Elizabeth. She's so good at *everything* she does."

"Elizabeth has quite a few fans," Mr. Edwards replied. "I heard a lot of cheering when I made the announcement."

"That's because she's always so helpful and nice to people," Jessica said. "She's a *model* for the rest of us."

"I thoroughly agree." Mr. Edwards grinned and waved. "See you tomorrow, Jessica."

Jessica beamed. Bruce Patman might *think* he had a chance of being named Model Student, but she knew better. Elizabeth had the nomination all sewn up—and it was all because Jessica had waged a winning campaign! As she headed for the Dairi Burger to meet the Unicorns, Jessica considered a possible future career for herself. Jessica Wakefield, Campaign Manager.

* * *

Elizabeth was getting some books out of her locker after school when Pamela came up to her. She was wearing neatly pressed khakis, a plaid blouse, and loafers. She had also tied her short dark hair into a ponytail. Elizabeth felt as if she were looking at a carbon copy of herself.

"Hi, Elizabeth. I guess you heard about the Model Student competition. I've been thinking about it all day," Pamela said seriously. "I think that *you're* the best candidate."

"Thanks, Pamela," Elizabeth said, kneeling down to put her books into her backpack. "I appreciate the compliment."

"I want to organize a sort of write-in campaign for you," Pamela continued.

Elizabeth stood up. "A write-in campaign?"

"You know," Pamela said, "like in an election. We'll write up a statement to Mr. Clark saying that you're the best possible candidate, and we'll get kids to sign it."

Elizabeth stared at Pamela. "You can't be serious!"

"Why not?" Pamela asked. "Bruce Patman's already on the campaign trail. In fact, he told me that Coach Cassels is going to nominate him and that he's sure that a lot of other teachers will vote for him, too. We have to get your name out there right away!"

Elizabeth slammed her locker shut. "Forget it, Pamela," she said firmly. "I don't want my name on any petition."

"But I—I don't see why not," Pamela sputtered.

"*Because*, that's why," Elizabeth said as she slung her backpack over her shoulder. "Sorry, Pamela, but I have to go. I promised Todd I'd meet him at the basketball court."

Pamela trailed along behind her. "But Elizabeth—" she protested.

Elizabeth began to walk faster. "No petitions. OK?"

"OK," Pamela said reluctantly. She cupped her hands around her mouth as Elizabeth turned the corner. "But I still think you're the perfect Model Student," she called.

"The perfect Model Student?" Todd asked as Elizabeth came up to him. "What was all that about?"

"Pamela has this nutty idea about starting a petition," Elizabeth said. "She wants me to run for Model Student."

Todd laughed. "A petition may be overdoing

it," he said, "but Pamela's on the right track. You'd be a great candidate."

"Thanks," she said sincerely. Coming from Todd, the compliment meant a lot.

Todd grinned. "We haven't celebrated your winning the *Teen Scene* contest yet. How about an ice cream cone, my treat?"

"That would be terrific!" As they went off together, Elizabeth couldn't help feeling that she was the luckiest girl in Sweet Valley.

Three

◇

On Tuesday morning, Jessica was walking into school when Aaron Dallas, the boy she had a crush on, joined her. "Hi, Jessica," he said. "Hey, did you hear? Coach Cassels has definitely decided to nominate Bruce for Model Student."

Jessica frowned. "Who told you that?" she asked. She knew that Bruce could never win over Elizabeth on merit, but he did have a lot of influence.

"Bruce did," Aaron replied. "It's a good thing, too. Bruce is in big trouble with his father. But I'm sure his father will calm down if Bruce wins."

Jessica's heart sank. If Bruce had a *real* reason

for wanting to be Model Student, he would be trying very hard to get the nomination. She would have to try even harder to get Elizabeth nominated.

In homeroom that morning, Jessica bounced into action again. Belinda Layton came up to Mr. Davis's desk, where Jessica was standing. "Mr. Davis," she said, "I have a question about the Model Student competition. Is being involved with sports as good as being involved with art? As far as the contest is concerned, I mean." Belinda was the star player on the school softball team and one of Jessica's fellow Unicorns.

"Good question, Belinda," Mr. Davis said. "No, one activity is not better than another. I think the most important thing is that a Model Student is involved in many different activities."

"Like the newspaper," Jessica suggested.

Mr. Davis nodded. "Yes," he said.

"Or writing contests," Jessica went on.

Mr. Davis nodded again.

"Or being a Junior Journalist," Jessica said triumphantly.

"Thank you, Jessica," Mr. Davis said. "I think I get your point." He rapped on his desk to bring the class to order. Jessica took her seat. Now Mr. Davis would be sure to think of Elizabeth when it was time to nominate the Model Student! Bruce Patman didn't stand a chance.

Elizabeth was leaving homeroom that morning when Amy, Julie, Brooke Dennis, and Maria Slater joined her. "We just overheard a couple of kids talking about you. They were saying that you should be nominated as Model Student. And I agree," Amy said.

"I do, too," Maria said. "And I'll bet that a lot of teachers think so, too."

Elizabeth smiled. "It would certainly be an honor," she said. "But there are plenty of other people who should be nominated, like Belinda. And Todd. He's a really good student, *and* he's the star of the basketball team."

Amy grinned. "And Bruce Patman. There's a rumor going around that Coach Cassels is nominating him. But I'm rooting for you, Elizabeth."

"I am, too," Brooke said.

Julie grinned. "See? It's unanimous."

"Right," Amy said. "And I'll bet Pamela would vote for you, too. In fact, she's probably working on a big banner for you."

Maria giggled. "I heard she's taking out a full-page ad in the *Sixers*."

"And I heard she's renting a sky-writing plane to write 'Elizabeth Wakefield Is the Greatest' over the freeway," Julie said.

Elizabeth tried to smile. *They don't know how close they are to the truth about Pamela*, she thought.

Jessica and Grace Oliver were standing in the library in front of Ms. Luster's desk when Bruce Patman walked past them with a couple of his friends. "I hear Bruce Patman is going to be nominated for that Model Student contest," Grace whispered.

Jessica glanced at Ms. Luster, who was busy checking out books. It looked as though she might be listening. Now was as good a time as any to torpedo Bruce's chances.

"Anybody who knows Bruce knows he's not a serious candidate," Jessica said confidently. "I bet he does three or four detentions a month. Nobody who does *any* detentions could be a Model Student."

"I guess you're right," Grace said. "Hey, how about Winston Egbert? He'd be good."

Jessica snickered. "Good at what?" she asked. "Good at being a nerd?" Winston was tall and slender, with brown hair and brown eyes and ears that turned bright red when he got embarrassed. Jessica was surprised to hear Grace even mention his name.

Ms. Luster looked up from the books she was checking out. "Next, please," she said.

Jessica stepped forward. "Hi, Ms. Luster," she said. "I want to check out these books."

"I'm glad to see you're reading more, Jessica," Ms. Luster said as she stamped the books.

"I'm trying to keep up with Elizabeth," she said dramatically, "but it's very hard. I could never read as much as *she* does. She's a *model* reader." Jessica leaned forward. "In fact, she's a *model* student, wouldn't you say?"

Ms. Luster looked slightly amused. "Yes, Elizabeth is one of my very best customers," she replied. "Next, please."

Jessica smiled slyly as she left the library. *Bruce Patman,* she thought, *eat your heart out.*

That afternoon after school, Elizabeth went to Mr. Bowman's room to work on the *Sixers.* She turned the knob, but the door did not budge.

Elizabeth frowned. Mr. Bowman had an open-door policy. His door was never locked to students, and he was expecting her to come by and do some work on the newspaper now. She raised her hand to knock.

At that moment, Elizabeth heard low voices coming from the room. "Elizabeth is the best student I have," she heard Mr. Bowman say. "She's more mature than most of the eighth graders. She's the one I'd nominate."

Elizabeth dropped her hand and took a quick step backward. She looked around hurriedly, hoping that nobody had seen her. Then she turned and started to walk away as fast as she could. She had not meant to eavesdrop on Mr. Bowman's private conversation. She felt guilty and embarrassed, having overheard a compliment she obviously was not meant to hear.

She was halfway down the hall when she heard Mr. Bowman's door open and close. She glanced quickly over her shoulder. The man who was leaving the room was the principal, Mr. Clark—the one who was ultimately responsible for nominating Sweet Valley Middle School's Model Student!

Elizabeth leaned against a locker, feeling her breath coming fast and her heart pounding. Mr. Bowman had told Mr. Clark that she was his best student! And then he had said that she was the one he would nominate. The only thing he could have been talking about was the Model Student competition!

Forgetting all about her plan to work on the *Sixers*, Elizabeth started home. She was lost in her thoughts about the Model Student competition. *If Mr. Bowman's going to nominate me*, she thought, *I'd better figure out exactly what a Model Student is!*

When Elizabeth got home, she raced up to Jessica's room. She sat down on Jessica's bed and kicked off her loafers. Jessica eyed her curiously. Elizabeth's eyes were shining, and her cheeks were rosy pink. A smile played around the corners of her mouth.

"You look like you're about to burst," Jessica said. "What's up?"

Elizabeth pulled her knees under her chin and wrapped her arms around them. "It's a secret, sort of," she said. "But everybody will know in a few days."

"Well, then, what is it?" she demanded. "Does it have something to do with Todd?"

Elizabeth smiled mysteriously. "It has something to do with *me*," she said. "Mr. Bowman is going to nominate me to be Sweet Valley Middle

School's Model Student. Can you believe it, Jessica?''

Jessica smiled smugly. "Actually, yes," she said. "I *can* believe it. I mean, I'm not at all surprised, Elizabeth. *Everybody* thinks you're perfect. Nobody deserves the nomination more than you."

Elizabeth sighed. "Well, *I* can't believe it. Not yet, anyway. It still seems too good to be true. Ever since the contest was announced, Amy and Pamela have been predicting that I'd be named Model Student. But I didn't really believe them. After all, they're both pretty biased. But now that I've heard it from Mr. Bowman, I *know* it's true."

Jessica grinned. "You mean, you really thought you weren't good enough to qualify as Model Student?"

Elizabeth tilted her head thoughtfully. "Well, yes. I've always considered myself to be an average person. I mean, I like riding bikes and going to the beach. I like eating hamburgers and hanging out with Todd." She grinned. "Pretty average stuff, huh?"

"Yeah, but you're leaving out a lot of other stuff," Jessica said. "You get top grades, you're editor of the *Sixers*, and you were chosen to be Junior Journalist. And you're the first-prize winner in the *Teen Scene* essay contest! What's average about that?"

Elizabeth smiled. "Well, since you put it that way," she said, "maybe I'm not as average as I thought."

"Did Mr. Bowman come right out and tell you after school?" Jessica did not think Mr. Bowman would have told Elizabeth about her campaigning, but she wanted to be sure.

Elizabeth colored. "No," she said. "I—I overheard him talking to Mr. Clark. It's not official yet," she added quickly, "so maybe we'd better not tell anybody."

"Not tell anybody! Don't be silly, Elizabeth! Everybody already suspects that you'll be the Model Student. Anyway, it's such a terrific secret! Caroline Pearce is bound to get her hands on it, and if she does, she'll mess it up somehow. It'd be better if she gets it from one of us, so she gets the real story for a change."

"But maybe other teachers will nominate other kids," Elizabeth protested weakly. "I mean, it's not a sure thing. It would be awful if everybody started talking about *me*, and the Model Student turned out to be somebody else."

Jessica hid a smile. Elizabeth did not know

that all the other teachers were on her side, too. *She* had seen to that. "So what if they do nominate other kids?" she said. "We won't say that you're going to be *the* one Mr. Clark chooses. We'll just say you've been nominated, and we won't say where we've heard it. Anyway, we'll let Caroline make up a source, and then you'll be off the hook. OK?"

Elizabeth frowned. "Well, when you put it like that," she said slowly, "I guess it's OK." She closed her eyes and took a deep breath. "I still can't believe it, Jessica."

Jessica bounced off the bed. "Mom's in the kitchen, and I heard Dad's car just before you came in. Let's go tell them!"

Mrs. Wakefield was taking a potato salad out of the refrigerator, and Mr. Wakefield was making hamburger patties. Steven was lounging at the kitchen table, munching on an apple.

"Guess what happened to Elizabeth!" Jessica cried as she barged into the kitchen. Elizabeth trailed along behind her.

"She got a hundred on her history test," Mrs. Wakefield guessed.

"Did you?" Jessica asked.

Elizabeth smiled. "Yes, but it's something better."

Mr. Wakefield began to stack the patties on a plate. "Better than a hundred on a history test?" he mused. "Well, it must be something *really* special. Did you win another writing contest, Elizabeth?"

"Better than that, even!" Jessica exclaimed. "Steven, what's your guess?"

"She got named Girl of the Century?" Steven asked through a mouth full of apple.

Jessica laughed. "You're close, Steven. Elizabeth's being nominated as Sweet Valley Middle School's Model Student. Every middle school in the country gets to nominate at least one person, and Elizabeth's ours!"

"Elizabeth!" Mrs. Wakefield said. "This is wonderful news!"

Mr. Wakefield grinned. "We've known all along that you're a model daughter—now a model student, too!"

"It hasn't really happened yet," Elizabeth cautioned.

"But Mr. Bowman told Mr. Clark that he's going to nominate you," Jessica reminded her.

"And all the kids at school think that you're the perfect candidate."

Steven examined his apple core. "Well," he said thoughtfully, "I guess if I had to nominate a Model Student, Elizabeth would definitely be in the top five."

"The top *five!*" Jessica said heatedly. "And just who are the other four?"

Steven frowned. "Well, there's . . ." He paused and his frown deepened. "And of course, there's . . ."

"You see?" Jessica said triumphantly. "You can't name anybody else. Elizabeth is *the* one!"

Steven shrugged and grinned at Elizabeth. "I guess you're it, Shrimp. Good job."

"Well, we can't go out for another celebration dinner because we've already started the grill. But how about going out for ice cream after dinner?" Mrs. Wakefield suggested.

"Fantastic," Jessica said.

Elizabeth nodded. Jessica thought her sister still looked as if she couldn't quite believe what had happened.

Four

◇

Elizabeth woke up early on Wednesday morning with goosebumps all over her arms. She had just had a crazy but wonderful dream. She had dreamed that she was standing on the stage in the auditorium at school, wearing her best dress and a lacy crown of pink and white flowers. In front of her were rows and rows of students and teachers, cheering and shouting, "Elizabeth! Elizabeth!" Ms. Langberg, with a huge megaphone in her hand, led the cheering, while the school band played "Hail to the Chief." Mr. Clark had just handed her a big proclamation, printed on a parchment scroll. In fancy lettering it read, "We the students and teachers of Sweet Valley Middle School do hereby proclaim *Elizabeth Wakefield* as our Model Student. Long may she reign!"

Elizabeth laughed out loud. It was a silly dream, but it left her with an incredible feeling of anticipation. Maybe she would not really be selected Model Student or receive a fancy parchment scroll. But Mr. Bowman, her favorite teacher, thought she was the most mature and the best qualified of all his students. That in itself was terrific.

Elizabeth jumped out of bed and hurried into the bathroom to brush her teeth. She could hear Jessica turning over in her bed, and she called out, "Good morning, Jessica!"

A minute later, Jessica appeared at the bathroom door in her pajamas, sleepily rubbing her eyes. "It's still dark," she said. "What time is it?"

"It's only six-thirty," Elizabeth replied cheerfully, "but I thought I'd get an early start. I have some important reading to do."

"I think I'll get a late start, if it's all the same to you," Jessica said, heading back to bed. "See you at breakfast."

Elizabeth hurried back into her room and

stood in front of the closet. Today was an important day. Last night she had told Jessica that it was all right to tell other people about her nomination, which meant that in a few hours *everybody* would know. They would all be watching her, and that meant she had to show them what a Model Student looked like.

The night before, she had laid out her tan corduroys and a blue striped shirt, but now the outfit did not seem quite right. Cords and stripes were certainly neat and tidy, but they were not dignified enough. Elizabeth reached into the back of her closet and pulled out the navy-blue skirt that she had gotten for the choir concert and had never worn again, and a pair of navy flats. Then she added a navy ribbon to her hair and tucked it into a bun. *It's perfect!* Elizabeth whispered to herself.

For the next forty-five minutes, Elizabeth studied the Model Student Guide, reading every paragraph until she knew it almost by heart. She didn't want to make any mistakes on her first day as a Model Student, but all this reading was making her very hungry. Finally, she went downstairs for breakfast.

Jessica was eating a bowl of cornflakes. When she saw Elizabeth, she almost choked. "Elizabeth, what in the *world* are you wearing?"

"Just a skirt and blouse," Elizabeth replied casually. "Do you like it?"

Jessica giggled. "If you want to know the truth, you look like a librarian."

For a moment, Elizabeth was offended. Then she remembered that the Guide said that a Model Student was friendly and cheerful. "Thank you," she said calmly as she went to the refrigerator to get the orange juice.

"Thank you?" Jessica repeated. "I tell you that you look like a librarian, and you say *thank you*?"

Elizabeth just smiled.

Steven came into the kitchen whistling the Sweet Valley High fight song. He stopped in mid-note when he saw Elizabeth. "Whose funeral are you going to?" he asked.

Elizabeth lifted her chin. The Guide gave no tips about how a Model Student should behave toward an obnoxious brother. But she thought that the authors of the Guide would probably not approve of her getting into a fight with him. "Good morning, Steven," she said pleasantly.

Steven rolled his eyes and shook his head. Then, grabbing a doughnut and an orange, he headed for the door.

"I've got to go, too," Jessica said. "I promised Lila I'd meet her before school." She pointed to the last doughnut. "I'll split it with you."

"That's OK," Elizabeth said, remembering that a Model Student ate a balanced diet, which probably meant that she did not eat a lot of sugar. "You take it."

"Thanks!" Jessica grabbed the doughnut and dashed out the door. A moment later she peeked back in. "If I can find Caroline Pearce, I'll tell her about the nomination. OK?"

"OK," Elizabeth said. But when Jessica had gone again, she felt a twinge of guilt. She had never started a rumor about herself before, and she did not feel right about it. Maybe she should have told Jessica to keep quiet for a while. But then she pushed the guilt away. Everybody was expecting her to be nominated, and anyway, the truth would come out in a day or two. What was the point in keeping it a big secret?

When Elizabeth got to school that morning, she found out that Jessica had already told Caroline. Caroline, in turn, had gone around telling everybody she saw, including Pamela.

"Elizabeth!" Pamela shrieked. "I'm so *glad!*"

"It's not definite yet," Elizabeth said.

"It's just a matter of time." Pamela tossed her head confidently. "Elizabeth, I just *love* your outfit. You look exactly like a Model Student!"

Elizabeth smiled gratefully. It was nice of Pamela to compliment her on her outfit, particularly after what Jessica and Steven had said about it.

Just then, Amy and Julie came rushing up to join them. "We just heard," Julie said, breathless. "It's wonderful, Elizabeth!"

"It's not definite yet," Elizabeth cautioned automatically.

"It'll happen," Amy said positively. Then she looked closely at Elizabeth. "What did you do to your hair?"

"I think it looks very nice that way," Pamela said.

Amy snorted. "That bun makes you look like a bookworm!"

"I like your ribbon," Julie said tactfully. "It's—uh, it's a nice touch."

"Congratulations again," Todd said as he

joined the girls. "I just heard the news from Caroline. I'm really glad for you, Elizabeth." Then he cocked an eyebrow. "Hey, why's your hair skinned back like that? It makes you look like a librarian."

Amy laughed. "See? What did I tell you?"

Elizabeth tried to smile. A Model Student probably would not be bothered by a few critical remarks, even when they came from people she liked as much as Todd and Amy. But when she and Pamela were walking off a few minutes later, she said, "Maybe I should take my hair down. Nobody likes it this way."

"*I* like it," Pamela said. "Leave it up, Elizabeth. If some people don't like it, that's *their* problem."

Elizabeth smiled at Pamela. At least she had *somebody* on her side.

For the rest of the morning, kids came up to Elizabeth to congratulate her and to tell her how happy they were that she was being nominated. Over and over she said to them, "It's not certain yet." But everyone seemed to think that her nomination was definite.

"They all *know* you're going to be nominated, Elizabeth," Pamela pointed out. "You don't have to keep reminding them that it's not official yet."

"I guess you're right," Elizabeth answered. The next time somebody congratulated her, she just said, "Thanks."

At lunch, Elizabeth sat with the staff of the *Sixers* so that they could look over the latest edition of the newspaper. Mr. Bowman had pointed out that there were several typographical errors. And then he had pointed out something even worse. Two captions had gotten switched. The caption HOME TEAM STRIKES OUT appeared under a picture of Mr. Edwards giving a Certificate of Merit to the three cafeteria cooks, while LOVE THOSE COOKIES! appeared under a photo of heavy-set Dennis Cookman, the softball team's relief pitcher, striking out.

Elizabeth frowned. She'd always let the staff editors—Amy, Patrick Morris, and Nora Mercandy—do the last-minute check of the copy before the paper was printed. A few errors slipped into every issue, but Elizabeth usually wasn't bothered by them. But today, she felt self-conscious about everything—including the *Sixers*. She had the feeling that a Model Student would not let errors creep into a newspaper she edited. A Model Student would make sure that the copy was perfect before it was printed. Besides, what if Mr. Bowman decided *not* to nominate her because of the errors?

"Maybe we'd better discuss this problem at our meeting this afternoon," she said.

Amy and Nora nodded in agreement. "Sure," Patrick said. He looked down at the pictures and laughed. "But you have to admit that the mistake is pretty funny."

"Yeah," Amy said with a giggle. "What a coincidence. I mean, Cookie *is* Dennis Cookman's nickname!"

"I don't think it's funny," Elizabeth said stiffly.

Patrick, Nora, and Amy all turned to Elizabeth at the same time. "What's a mistake or two?" Amy asked. "Whoever spots it probably will just get a good laugh. In fact, I'll bet they think we did it on purpose!"

As Elizabeth was leaving the cafeteria after lunch, Pamela McDonald caught up with her. Pamela had eaten lunch at a table near Elizabeth's, and she'd overheard the conversation among the *Sixers* staff.

"I'm proud of you for sticking to your guns, Elizabeth," Pamela said.

Elizabeth nodded. "Well, the newspaper *is*

my responsibility. I'm the one people will blame when there are errors."

"You're a hundred percent right, Elizabeth," Pamela assured her. "Maybe you should tell them that from now on you have to approve everything that goes into the paper, in writing, *before* it's printed."

"I don't know if that would work," Elizabeth said thoughtfully. "It would be a big nuisance for everyone to show me all their last-minute changes. And I don't know if I've got the time to check *everything*. I've always relied on the others to check their own copy."

"But that's why there's a problem," Pamela pointed out. "I'll bet if *you* checked, *you'd* find all the errors!"

Elizabeth thought about Pamela's suggestion all through her afternoon classes. And the more she thought about it, the more she liked the idea. If she had the responsibility, she should have the authority, too.

Elizabeth began the *Sixers* meeting that afternoon by going over the stories they were preparing for the upcoming issues. Then Mr. Bowman surprised her by suggesting that they reprint her prize-winning essay.

Elizabeth was very flattered that her essay was going to be reprinted, and she was glad that the staff was enthusiastic about running it. But their enthusiasm did not change her decision to take complete control of the paper. Her new plan would cause the newspaper staff a little extra trouble, but she was sure it was the right thing to do.

When Mr. Bowman left the room, Elizabeth stood up.

"I have an announcement," she said firmly, "about a change in the way we do things. Too many errors have been creeping into the copy. So from now on, the editor has to approve everything that goes into the paper. In *writing*."

Amy gasped. "Everything? You mean, all those little-bitty last-minute changes that we make in our pieces?"

"Everything," Elizabeth said emphatically. "Obviously, whoever checked the copy the last time didn't do a very good job." Elizabeth had not meant to say it quite so bluntly, but it was too late to take the words back.

"I did the best I could," Nora said defensively. She pushed her long black hair back away from her face. "I guess I just got careless and missed the captions. I'll be more careful next time."

Elizabeth felt her lips tighten, but she managed a small smile. "Next time, you won't have to worry, Nora," she said reassuringly. "*I'll* take care of the final checking." Nora's face darkened, but Elizabeth ignored her. "Now, does anybody have any questions about the new procedure?"

"Can't we discuss this, Elizabeth?" Julie Porter pleaded. "Those mixed-up captions were the first big problem we've ever had. Aren't we overreacting to something pretty minor?"

"Definitely not," Elizabeth said decisively. "An error is an error, Julie. We simply can't afford to let it happen again. Now, if nobody has any other questions," she said, gathering her papers busily, "we're finished with our meeting."

After everyone else had gone, Amy came up to Elizabeth. "Elizabeth," she said, "try to see things from *our* point of view. Getting your approval is going to mean a lot of extra work for us, *and* it'll be tough for you to check every piece of copy at the last minute. Don't forget that you'll also have to check everything written by the occasional staffers."

Elizabeth sighed. Why couldn't Amy understand *her* side of things, as Pamela did? "Try to see it from *my* point of view," she said. "It's important to get things *right*."

Amy folded her arms across her chest. "So important that you have to upset people?" she asked indignantly.

"Who's upset?"

"Nora, for one," Amy replied. "You made it sound as if you have to take things over because *she* messed up. And Patrick, for another. I heard him say to Sophia, 'Who does she think she is— Queen Elizabeth?' "

Elizabeth sighed again. "I'm sorry that Nora and Patrick feel that way," she said.

"Elizabeth," Amy said, "you're being absolutely *impossible*." And without another word, she turned and walked away.

As Elizabeth left school that day, she was frowning. Had she done the right thing by changing the procedure? She had not meant to upset Nora or Patrick—or Amy, either. Maybe she *had* been a little out of line.

Just as Elizabeth was about to decide that she definitely *had* gone too far, Pamela popped up behind her.

"Hi, Elizabeth," she said. "I've been waiting for you. What did the staff think about your plan?"

"It didn't go over very well," Elizabeth admitted. "In fact, everybody seemed pretty upset by the idea—even Amy." She sighed. "Maybe it was the way I presented it."

"No way," Pamela said. "If they didn't like it, it's because they don't like the idea of taking orders, that's all. You want the *Sixers* to be the very best newspaper possible. And it *can* be the very best, under your leadership." She paused, then added, "Really, Elizabeth, everybody could benefit from following your example."

Elizabeth smiled. Yes, it *was* important that the *Sixers* be the very best newspaper. No Model Student would settle for anything less! "Thanks, Pamela," Elizabeth said gratefully. It was nice to have at least *one* friend who appreciated how important it was to get things right!

Five

◇

Jessica spent Thursday afternoon with Lila and Ellen shopping at the mall. By the time she got home, she was worn out from helping Lila try on dozens of outfits, choose several pairs of shoes, and decide which accessories to buy. It had been a *hard* afternoon. And she'd had a hard morning, too. She had talked to several teachers that she had not had a chance to speak to the day before, and everyone had agreed that Elizabeth would be a good candidate for Model Student.

Jessica took some cookies and a soda to her room. She was lying on her bed with her eyes closed when Elizabeth came into her room.

"Hi," Elizabeth said. She looked at Jessica sympathetically. "You look worn out. Madame André must have made you work pretty hard at ballet class today."

Jessica opened one eye. "I played hooky from ballet," she said. "I went shopping with Lila and Ellen. Lila got a bonus on her allowance, and she wanted us to help her spend it. It was a lot of work."

Elizabeth shook her head. "Really, Jessica," she said sternly.

Jessica opened both eyes. "Really what?" she asked. "What's wrong with going shopping?"

"What's wrong," Elizabeth explained patiently, "is that shopping is a waste of time, especially when you skipped ballet class to do it. What do you have to show for your afternoon?"

Jessica propped herself up on her elbows and thought for a minute. "Let's see," she said. "Lila's got a new purple top and three new skirts and a silver pendant, and"—she wiggled her bare toes— "I've got sore feet."

Elizabeth sighed. "You'd have been better off if you'd gotten your sore feet at Madame André's dance studio."

"Elizabeth," Jessica said warily. "Is something bothering you?"

"Bothering me?" Elizabeth asked. "What gave you that idea?"

"You seem—well, different," Jessica said carefully.

"I'm concerned about *you*, Jess. I'm concerned that you spend too much of your time hanging around with the Unicorns."

"But I *like* the Unicorns," Jessica protested mildly. What had gotten into Elizabeth? She was acting like a fussy old grandmother. "And we weren't hanging around. We were *shopping*."

"What you need are a few worthwhile hobbies," Elizabeth said with a firm nod of her head. "And shopping doesn't qualify. You need some *enriching* hobbies."

Jessica burst into laughter. "Enriching hobbies?" she hooted. "Come off it, Lizzie!"

Jessica smothered a smile. It suddenly occurred to her what was behind Elizabeth's bossiness! "It's nice of you to be concerned about me, Elizabeth," Jessica said. "But I don't think I'm Model Student material."

"That has nothing to do with it. *Everyone*

should have a hobby that will increase their self-discipline and build their cultural interests. Ballet is very cultural, but it would be good for you to take up something for recreation, like a game."

Jessica snickered. "What did you have in mind? Checkers? Tic-tac-toe?"

"There's chess," Elizabeth replied seriously. "Chess demands discipline, and it's *very* cultural. Or you could take up a musical instrument, like the cello or the harp."

"The *harp*?" Jessica burst into laughter again. "Plucking all those strings would probably wreck my nails! Listen, Elizabeth," Jessica said. "I'm *myself,* and I'm satisfied with the way I am. I *like* to waste time. I love shopping with the Unicorns and talking on the phone and going to parties. Remember that prize-winning essay you wrote about how important it is to be an individual? Well, maybe I don't have a lot of self-discipline, and maybe I'm not the most cultured person in the world. But I'm an *individual,* and I'm happy."

"It's my turn to set the table, so I'd better go." Elizabeth headed toward the door. Then she turned and gave her twin a warm, encouraging smile. "Being satisfied with yourself isn't good enough. You have to try to be better."

Jessica laid back down on her bed and sighed. "Maybe. But if being better means enjoying life less, you can count me out, Elizabeth."

Early Friday morning, Jessica was still sleeping soundly when Elizabeth came into her room and sat on her bed.

"Wake up, Jessica," she said, shaking her sister's shoulder.

"Whatever it is, it can wait until dawn," Jessica said sleepily, burrowing under the covers.

"Pamela McDonald and I are going jogging," Elizabeth said. "Want to come along?"

Jessica opened one eye and saw that Elizabeth was wearing her yellow sweats and her running shoes. "But you can't run in the dark," she objected. "You'll fall on your face."

"It's not *that* dark," Elizabeth said. "Anyway, we're just running around the block ten or fifteen times."

"Ten or fifteen times!" Jessica squawked. "Are you crazy?"

"Come on, Jessica," Elizabeth urged. "It'll be

good for you. Really, you need to get more exercise. All you do is lie around."

"But people are *supposed* to lie around—at least until dawn," Jessica objected, pulling the pillow over her head. "I'll exercise after the sun comes up."

Jessica had forgotten to set her alarm, and it was past seven-thirty when she finally came downstairs dressed for school. She was pouring her cereal when Elizabeth came through the back door. She was wearing a plaid skirt and a primlooking blue blouse, and was carrying a tray of dirty dishes.

"I thought you were going jogging with Pamela," Jessica said, helping herself to orange juice.

"I did," Elizabeth said. She began to rinse off the dishes in the sink and to put them into the dishwasher. "We ran around the block fourteen times. You should have come along, Jess. It was very invigorating."

"I'll bet," Jessica said dryly. "The mere *thought* is invigorating." She glanced at the dirty dishes. "What else have you been doing?"

"I fixed breakfast for Mrs. Howard," Elizabeth replied, turning on the dishwasher. "She's got the flu, you know." The Howards were their next-door neighbors. "Mr. Howard's away on business," Elizabeth continued. "And Mrs. Howard is all alone."

Jessica pushed back her chair and stood up. All of a sudden she wasn't hungry anymore. "I think I'd better be on my way to school," she said.

"If you'll wait a second until I finish cleaning the kitchen, I'll walk with you," Elizabeth said. She wiped out the sink and rinsed the sponge. "I don't want to leave any chores for Mom when she comes home from work this afternoon."

Jessica sighed. "Perish the thought."

That afternoon after school, Lila invited the Unicorns to spend the afternoon sitting around her pool listening to tapes, and catching up on the latest gossip. Jessica was enjoying herself until Mandy reminded her it was time to go.

"It's my week to set the table." Mandy sighed. "If I don't get home soon, I'll be in *deep* trouble."

Jessica made a sour face. "Yeah, it's my turn, too," she said. She stretched lazily and reached for another chip. "But I don't have to leave this minute."

Of all the chores Jessica had to do, setting the table was the one she detested most. She didn't look forward to going home to do such a boring job. But when Jessica got home that afternoon, armed with a perfect alibi for not being home in time, she found that the table was already set. Elizabeth had laid out the Wakefields' best china and silver, folded the napkins into flowers, polished the silver candlesticks, and set a pretty bowl of red and orange zinnias in the middle of the table.

"Doesn't it look nice?" Elizabeth asked as she surveyed the table with a look of satisfaction.

"I guess," Jessica said, astonished. She should have been relieved that she had not been stuck setting the table, but oddly enough, she was not. It was hard to explain, but she felt outdone— as she had this morning, when Elizabeth had thought of taking breakfast to Mrs. Howard. By the time Elizabeth did *her* good deeds, there were none left for Jessica to do!

"Just wait until you taste my dessert," Elizabeth said. "I just finished making it from a recipe I found in a health-food magazine."

Jessica's spirits perked up. Dessert was her favorite part of the meal. "What is it?" she asked.

"Wait and see," Elizabeth said mysteriously. "It's a surprise."

It *was* a surprise, too, when Elizabeth finally brought the dessert to the table that evening. "Well, here it is," she said proudly. She began to spoon it out of the serving bowl into small dessert bowls. Jessica and Steven stared at it. They'd never seen anything like it before.

Mr. Wakefield set down his coffee cup and cleared his throat. "It looks very . . . interesting," he said carefully as he looked down at the brown mound speckled with darker brown bits. "What is it?"

"It's brown-rice pudding with raisins," Elizabeth replied, handing a bowl to Steven and one to Jessica. "It's very healthy." Her sister's tone reminded Jessica of Mrs. Gerhart, their cooking teacher.

Steven frowned down at his plate. "I don't care how healthy it is," he said. "Brown rice is *not* for dessert."

Jessica was glad that she had had a double helping of lasagna. She didn't want to hurt Elizabeth's feelings, but she agreed with Steven. Rice was definitely *not* for dessert, even if it did have raisins in it.

"I think it would be good for you to eat Elizabeth's dessert, Steven," his mother said gently, pouring another cup of coffee for herself and one for Mr. Wakefield. "Who knows? You might develop a liking for it. And Elizabeth's right— brown rice *is* nutritious."

At that moment, the telephone rang. Jessica usually made sure she got to the phone first when it rang during dinner, but this time Elizabeth beat her to it. Eagerly, Jessica cocked her ear, wondering if the call was for her.

It was. "Hello, Aaron," Jessica heard Elizabeth say.

Jessica pushed back her chair. She had been hoping Aaron would call. And she had promised Ellen that if he did call, she would phone her immediately and tell her everything.

But before Jessica could make a move for the phone, she heard Elizabeth say primly, "I'm terribly sorry, Aaron, but Jessica can't talk right now. She's eating dinner." And then, to Jessica's absolute horror, Elizabeth added, "Oh, and from now on, would you try not to call at dinnertime? Thank you. Good-bye."

Jessica gasped. Elizabeth had told Aaron *not* to call? How *could* she!

Elizabeth came back to the table and sat down to her brown-rice pudding. "I really think," she said to Jessica, "that it would be better if we asked our friends to call us after the dinner hour."

"Did you read *that* in the Model Student Guide, too?" Jessica asked crossly.

"No," Elizabeth said. She frowned seriously. "Why? Did you see it in there? Did I miss something?"

Steven snickered, and Jessica noticed that her mother and father were trading glances. Obviously, Jessica was not the only one who had noticed a change in Elizabeth.

As soon as Jessica could escape from her brown-rice pudding, she headed for the phone and called Aaron. But to her great disappointment, she found that he had just left for a camping trip with his father. She would not be able to talk to him all weekend. She trudged up the stairs to her room, her shoulders slumped, feeling terribly sorry for herself. After the way Elizabeth had lectured Aaron, she doubted he would *ever* call her back. He had probably made up his mind that she was a total nerd and that Elizabeth was a candidate for Sweet Valley Middle School's Model Loser!

Six

◈

Saturday was the day of the week that Jessica most looked forward to because that was the day she got to do exactly what she wanted. She could go shopping with the Unicorns, go to the beach, or just loaf around the house. This Saturday, she'd decided to start off by sleeping late. She gave Elizabeth strict orders not to wake her up early—not *even* to go jogging. When she finally got up, she didn't bother to get dressed. It was gray and foggy outside, and luckily, there was an old movie on TV starring Dolores Dufay, her all-time favorite actress. Jessica had once helped Miss Dufay, and in return, Miss Dufay had given Jessica some very good pointers on acting. Jessica planned to spend an enjoyable morning studying Dolores Dufay's famous acting techniques. Maybe later she would call Maria Slater and have a confidential talk, actress to actress.

Jessica turned on the television and quickly decided that a movie wasn't complete without popcorn. When she went into the kitchen to make some, she was surprised to see Elizabeth on her knees in front of the open refrigerator. She was wearing one of her mother's aprons, and she'd pulled her hair back into that awful-looking bun she'd worn all week.

"What are you doing?" Steven asked, coming in behind Jessica. "Saying prayers to the refrigerator gods?"

Elizabeth smiled at them. "Good morning," she said cheerfully. "I'm just cleaning out a few things." She gestured toward the kitchen garbage pail, which was overflowing with bottles and jars. "Steven, would you mind taking this junk food out to the trash for me?"

Steven glanced at the garbage pail. "Hey!" he demanded. "You're throwing out the chocolate syrup for my ice cream! It's not even empty! And the jelly doughnuts left over from yesterday—I was planning to have them for breakfast!" He pawed frantically through the garbage. "And here's the strawberry eclair I was saving . . ."

Jessica smothered a laugh, but Elizabeth wasn't amused. "Steven," she said with a frown, "I threw away all those things because they're not good for you. You're eating too much sugar."

Steven put the chocolate syrup back into the refrigerator and rescued his slightly squashed doughnuts. "I don't care whether this stuff is good for me or not," he said belligerently. "It's *mine*. What gives you the right to throw it away?"

Just then, Mrs. Wakefield entered the kitchen and glanced at what Elizabeth was doing. "How *thoughtful* of you, Elizabeth!" she exclaimed. "That refrigerator really needed a good cleaning."

"Mom," Steven complained, "tell her not to throw my good stuff away!"

"It's not good, Steven," Elizabeth argued. "I've *told* you. We're all eating too much sugar. We're turning into sugar junkies. We should give it up—and that includes desserts."

"Give up dessert!" Jessica shouted. "No way!"

"Children," Mrs. Wakefield said mildly, "let's not have any arguments until after I've had my morning coffee." She opened the coffee canister.

"That's odd," she said with a frown. "I could have sworn there was enough left for one more pot."

"Coffee?" Mr. Wakefield said, coming into the kitchen. "Did somebody mention coffee?" He sniffed. "Where is it? I don't smell it."

"You don't smell it, Dad," Elizabeth said, "because there isn't any." She opened the cupboard and took out a small box. "I thought it would be better if you drank this instead."

"What?" Mr. Wakefield exclaimed in surprise. "No coffee?"

Steven grinned. "Join the club, Dad. Elizabeth tried to trash my chocolate sauce, too."

"Coffee and chocolate are full of caffeine," Elizabeth said, folding her arms and frowning. "Caffeine is not good for you."

Mrs. Wakefield looked at the label on the box Elizabeth had given her. " 'Delicious, Healthy Herb Tea,' " she read. " 'Made from chicory root and dandelions.' "

"It has lots of vitamin A," Elizabeth announced.

"Dandelions!" Mr. Wakefield shook his head. "Sounds like rabbit food. If it's all the same to you, Elizabeth, I think I'll stick with my coffee. Now, where is it?''

Elizabeth looked crestfallen. She pulled the crumpled bag out of the garbage and handed it to her mother.

"Thank you, Elizabeth," Mrs. Wakefield said quietly. "From now on, I think you'd better check with other people before you throw away something they enjoy. If you'd like, you can help me plan our menus for next week to be sure we eat nutritious meals. But there will *definitely* be desserts."

"That's telling her, Mom," Steven cried. "And nix the brown-rice pudding, huh?"

Jessica couldn't decide whether to laugh at her twin or to feel sorry for her. Elizabeth had asked for it—acting as if she had the right to tell everybody what to eat. While her mother made coffee and Elizabeth finished cleaning out the refrigerator, Jessica got out the popcorn. As far as Jessica was concerned, popcorn was healthy, *even* for breakfast. When her popcorn was popped, she poured herself a glass of orange juice and went back into the den to watch her movie.

Elizabeth found her there a half-hour later,

stretched out on the floor in front of the TV, the almost-empty popcorn bowl at her elbow, her head propped up on sofa cushions.

Elizabeth stood between Jessica and the television. "What are you doing?" she asked.

"I'm eating popcorn and watching Dolores Dufay," Jessica replied. "Would you mind moving out of the way?"

Elizabeth gave Jessica a disapproving look. "Really, Jessica," she said, "you're still in your pajamas! It's a shame to waste an entire Saturday."

"I'm not wasting an *entire* Saturday," Jessica snapped, reaching for some more popcorn. "I'm only wasting the morning."

Elizabeth sniffed. "You should be improving your mind instead of filling it full of silly old movies."

"I'm improving my acting technique," Jessica retorted indignantly. "And this is *not* a silly old movie. It's Dolores Dufay's most famous film, and her big scene is about to come up. Please don't stand in front of the TV."

Elizabeth stepped aside. "Pamela and I are going to the museum to study that new exhibit of fossils. You should stop being a couch potato and come along."

"A couch potato isn't such a bad thing to be, especially on a foggy Saturday," Jessica said, her eyes glued to the TV. "Look, Elizabeth, doesn't Miss Dufay look absolutely fabulous? See that sad expression on her face? She's about to leave her sweetheart forever!"

Elizabeth sighed heavily. "I can't talk you into coming to the museum?" she asked.

"Forget it," Jessica said firmly, and Elizabeth left the den, shaking her head.

Jessica smiled and rearranged the sofa cushions. She knew that Elizabeth was thinking that her sister suffered from incurable mental laziness and would be a couch potato until the end of her days. But as far as Jessica was concerned, there were worse things in life than being a couch potato—being a Model Student, for one!

It drizzled on Sunday, just hard enough to keep Jessica from going to the open-air concert at Secca Lake with Ellen. Instead, she wrote a couple of paragraphs of her English essay, cleaned out a dresser drawer, and then sat down to read her latest fan magazine. She had read almost the entire magazine when she heard the doorbell ring. Remembering what had happened on Friday evening when Elizabeth had beaten her to the phone, Jessica raced downstairs. She didn't want Elizabeth to send away one of her friends.

"Hi," Amy said when Jessica opened the door. "I didn't have anything to do, so I thought I'd come over and see what you guys were up to."

"Nothing special," Jessica said, taking Amy's raincoat.

"Who's that at the door, Jessica?" Elizabeth called from the head of the stairs.

"It's Amy," Jessica replied.

"Tell her to come up," Elizabeth ordered.

Amy rolled her eyes. "Has she been like this all weekend?" she whispered.

"Worse," Jessica said. "She threw out my parents' coffee because she decided that caffeine wasn't good for them. And she tried to get me to go to the museum so I could improve my mind by studying fossils."

Amy nodded. "She asked me to go, too, but I don't really like Pamela. Her constant flattery is sickening."

Jessica laughed. She knew what Amy meant.

Elizabeth came to the top of the stairs again.

"What are you two whispering about?" she asked sharply. "Come on upstairs, Amy."

Jessica and Amy exchanged glances, and Jessica grinned. "If I can find the Monopoly set, we could play a game," she said. "How about that?"

"That's just what I was hoping you'd say," Amy replied, and they went upstairs. "Maybe a game will get Elizabeth's mind off being a Model Student."

"Hi, Amy," Elizabeth said when Jessica and Amy came into her room. "How about some Scrabble?"

"Amy would rather play Monopoly," Jessica said. She wasn't crazy about Scrabble. She wasn't as good a speller as Elizabeth was.

Elizabeth frowned. "Wouldn't you rather play Scrabble?" she asked Amy.

Amy glanced at Jessica and shrugged. "Yeah, I guess," she said. "I mean, it's not something I want to spend a lot of energy arguing about."

With a sigh, Jessica gave in, too. The three of them played a game of Scrabble. They were about to start the second game when Pamela arrived.

"Hi, Elizabeth," she said, ignoring Jessica and Amy. "Oh, you're playing Scrabble!"

"Want to play?" Elizabeth asked, and Amy grudgingly moved over to make room.

Pamela quickly sat down. "Oh, no, I could never play against *you*, Elizabeth. You're much too good a speller. Why, you're the most terrific speller I've ever met!"

Obviously pleased, Elizabeth smiled at Pamela. "I'm not that good, Pamela," she said modestly. "You're exaggerating."

"Yes, you are!" Pamela insisted. "You should be in the National Spelling Bee."

Amy glanced at Jessica and rolled her eyes. Pamela fawned all over Elizabeth, dishing out the compliments as quickly as Elizabeth could lap them up. But the more Pamela flattered Elizabeth, the more frustrated Amy got. Jessica could see her face getting redder and redder, and her pale gray eyes threw daggers at Pamela. The next time it was her turn, Amy put down her tiles with a triumphant "There!"

Pamela leaned forward. "B-A-L-O-N-E-Y," she spelled out. "I don't understand, Amy."

Amy dumped the rest of her tiles into the box and stood up. "It's what you've been giving Elizabeth all afternoon," she said. "It's your brand of flattery, and it makes me want to throw up!"

Jessica turned a snicker into a cough. Elizabeth looked up at Amy in shock. Pamela shook her head. "But I'm just telling the truth," she protested innocently.

Amy gave up and stormed out of the room and down the stairs.

Elizabeth started to get up to go after Amy, but Pamela pulled her down. "I think Amy is just jealous," she said knowingly. "It might be better if you left her alone for a while to think about what just happened."

"Jealous?" Elizabeth asked. "Jealous of *what*?"

Pamela shrugged. "Jealous of everything you've done," she said. "Jealous that you're the Model Student and she isn't. And she might be jealous of *us*, too," she added. "It must be pretty hard for her, knowing that she isn't your best friend anymore."

Suddenly, Jessica couldn't take it any longer, either. She stood up, dumping her tiles all over the board. "You can sit here and listen to this garbage all you want, Elizabeth," she said angrily. "But *I'm* sick and tired of it. Good-bye!"

Elizabeth shook her head. She felt confused. She and Amy had been friends for so long. Elizabeth thought she could predict how Amy would respond to almost anything. And she usually understood Jessica almost as well as Jessica understood herself. But right now, she was at a loss to explain why both of them had gotten so annoyed. "I just don't understand," she said.

"Well, I do," Pamela said. She picked up the scattered tiles and put them into the box. "They're *both* jealous."

"Do you really think so?" Elizabeth asked doubtfully.

"I really do," Pamela said with an emphatic nod. "It must be very hard for Jessica to see her twin getting so many wonderful honors when she doesn't get any herself. And neither Jessica nor Amy can even *begin* to appreciate how much of a strain this whole thing is for you, Elizabeth, or how hard it is to live up to everybody's expectations."

Elizabeth sighed. She momentarily wondered

if maybe Pamela's reasoning was a little off base. But why else would Amy and Jessica have run off like that? "I guess you're right," she said finally.

"Let's do something to get your mind off them," Pamela suggested.

"Like what?" Elizabeth asked as she put the Scrabble board back into the box.

"We could get your clothes ready for next week," Pamela said. "You're the center of attention. You want to be sure to look the part of the Model Student at all times. And you have such *terrific* clothes. I'd love to look through your closet."

"That's a great idea, Pamela," Elizabeth said enthusiastically. "We could make a list of everything I'm going to wear so I can be sure it will be clean and pressed. A Model Student always has a neat and tidy appearance."

For the next hour, Elizabeth and Pamela went through Elizabeth's closet, taking out blouses, skirts, and shoes, checking them over and putting aside those that needed attention. Pamela oohed and aahed over things she liked. At the end of the hour, Elizabeth had laid out all the clothes she would need for the week. Only one thing was missing—a blue blouse that she wanted to wear with her red plaid skirt.

It wasn't until after Pamela had gone that Elizabeth remembered she had loaned the missing blue blouse to Jessica a few weeks before. She went next door to Jessica's room.

"Jessica," she said, "I need my blue blouse. Where is it?"

Jessica glanced around. "It's here someplace," she said, looking at the rubble of clothes and magazines and papers that littered the floor. "It may take me a while to find it, though. You don't need it right this minute, do you?"

"No," Elizabeth admitted, "but I'd like to have it so I can wash it. Pamela and I made a list of all the clothes I'm wearing next week, and it's down for Tuesday's outfit."

Jessica sighed. "A list of clothes?"

"You know, Jessica," Elizabeth said, ignoring her sister's disbelief, "you wouldn't have any trouble finding my blouse if you cleaned your room once in a while. Really, I don't see how you live in this pigpen."

Jessica groaned. The old Elizabeth had sometimes teased her about her messy room, but that last remark came from the Model Student Monster.

Even though Jessica was angry at the way her twin was beginning to act, she knew she couldn't blame it all on Elizabeth. If she hadn't been so successful in her campaign to nominate Elizabeth, somebody else might have been chosen. If there was only some way to get Elizabeth to be her old self again!

Seven

◇

On Monday morning, Elizabeth got up bright and early and did thirty minutes of aerobics on the back deck before getting ready for school. She decided to wear the dark green skirt her mother had bought her when she was an usher for the school play and a tailored white blouse with a green cardigan, and once again she had pulled her hair back into a bun.

On the way to the kitchen for breakfast, she bumped into Steven. He chuckled when he saw her. "Where'd you get *that* outfit?" he asked. "You look like a refugee from a girls' boarding school."

Elizabeth pretended to ignore him, but his remark stung. She was glad when Pamela arrived to walk to school with her. Pamela always liked her clothes.

"You look really terrific, Elizabeth," Pamela said. "Green is a great color for you."

Elizabeth tossed her head and smiled. What did Steven know about girls' outfits?

"I see you've got your schedule, too," Pamela said, glancing at the clipboard Elizabeth held under her arm.

Elizabeth nodded. Pamela had suggested that she use a clipboard to keep track of daily events. Elizabeth thought it was a good idea, because a Model Student was always punctual and she liked the look of authority the clipboard gave her. Under her schedule she had fastened the Model Student Guide, for reference.

Elizabeth and Pamela had just walked through the main door at school when Caroline Pearce came rushing up to them. "Have you heard the latest?" she asked. "Mr. Clark is going to officially announce the Model Student nominee on Friday! I saw a notice on the bulletin board outside his office."

Elizabeth couldn't help but feel a little disappointed. Friday was a long way off. She'd have to wait an entire school week before she was officially named Model Student!

Elizabeth had just sat down in Mr. Bowman's English class that day when Randy Mason asked her a homework question. After she helped him, Winston Egbert came up to her. Jessica and the Unicorns might think Winston was a nerd, but Elizabeth liked him.

"I don't understand these verbs," Winston said, putting his workbook on Elizabeth's desk. "Can you help me?"

Elizabeth smiled. "Of course, Winston," she said warmly. "Sit down." For the few minutes before Mr. Bowman joined the class, Elizabeth showed Winston how to figure out the compound verbs in the sentences. As she handed him back his workbook, she said, "You probably shouldn't goof around during class so much."

Winston's ears turned neon pink, the way they always did when he was embarrassed. "I *try* to pay attention," he protested. "It's just that verbs are boring. Anyway, English isn't my best subject. I'm better in science."

"Being better in science doesn't help your

English grade," Elizabeth reminded Winston. As Winston got up, his ears still flaming, Elizabeth realized that he was hurt and embarrassed, and she almost felt sorry for having been so blunt with him. But part of her job as a Model Student was to help others see what they could gain by working hard and paying attention.

In Mrs. Arnette's social studies class later that morning, the students were discussing the book reports that were due in a few days. Each student was supposed to choose a book that portrayed an important aspect of American life. "I haven't been able to find a book I like," Ellen Riteman complained. "All the short books have been checked out."

Mrs. Arnette was about to respond to Ellen's complaint when Elizabeth spoke up. "I think you should do your report on *Tom Sawyer*, Ellen. The book tells a lot about nineteenth-century American life, and it's fun to read, too."

Mrs. Arnette beamed. "That's a very helpful suggestion, Elizabeth," she said. "There, you see, Ellen? Your problem is solved."

"But *Tom Sawyer* is a *long* book," Ellen complained, scowling at Elizabeth. "I'll never be able to read it in time to write the report."

"Of course you will," Elizabeth said encouragingly. "You never know what you're capable of doing until you've given yourself a chance. You just have to *try*."

Mrs. Arnette's smile grew broader. "That's the spirit, Elizabeth," she said as she waved her lesson plan book enthusiastically.

Ellen slid down in her seat and gave Elizabeth another dirty look, but Elizabeth just ignored it.

At lunch, Elizabeth found herself standing behind Janet Howell in the cafeteria line. Janet was an eighth grader and president of the Unicorn Club, and she was taking two pieces of cherry cheesecake for dessert.

Elizabeth moved a little closer. "Janet," she said, "there must be zillions of calories in that cheesecake, not to mention all the fat and sugar. You'd feel a lot healthier if you lost a few pounds."

Several Unicorns standing close by gave a collective gasp of shock. Janet turned around and fixed Elizabeth with an icy stare.

"I really think, Elizabeth," Janet said frostily, "that *you* would feel much happier if you kept your nose out of other people's affairs." Janet's voice rang out loud and clear, and several people turned to stare.

Elizabeth cleared her throat and looked down at her clipboard. She ran her finger down her schedule until she came to the lunch-hour time slot. "Excuse me," she said hastily. "I see I have to check out a few things for the *Sixers*." And she walked away quickly, glad that she had an excuse for getting away from Janet. She felt very uncomfortable when someone rejected her helpful advice.

Jessica was one of the people ahead of Janet in the cafeteria line. She had heard the whole exchange, but she hadn't turned around. She'd been too mortified. Now she bent over the salad bar, pretending she hadn't heard a thing.

"Jessica," Lila demanded crossly, "what in the world has gotten into Elizabeth? She's being utterly impossible."

"Right," Ellen chimed in. "You heard her insult Janet just now, and during cooking class this morning she insulted Lila."

Jessica sighed and took a bowl of cottage cheese from the salad bar. "I wish I knew. Actually, I think I *do* know," she said as she placed the bowl of cottage cheese on her tray. "It's this Model Student thing."

"I suppose that's why she's wearing that ridiculous green uniform and why she's been wearing her hair that way," Janet said with a scowl as she joined Jessica and the others.

Aaron, who had just finished paying for his lunch, joined the group. "And that's why she acted like a drill sergeant on the phone Friday night. She told me not to call at dinnertime anymore." He frowned. "How am I supposed to know when you're eating dinner, Jessica?"

Jessica bit her lip. Usually, when anybody— even one of the Unicorns—attacked Elizabeth, she loyally stood up for her. But right now she couldn't think of a single word to say in her twin's defense. Elizabeth's behavior these days was positively horrible.

"Well, Jessica, you can tell Elizabeth for me," Janet went on haughtily, "that she's gone *too far*. If I have any influence—and I believe I do—she won't be named Model Student. She'll be named Model Nerd!" Janet flounced off, holding her tray with the two slices of cherry cheesecake on it high.

Lila lifted her chin. "That goes ditto for me," she said. "The nerve of her, telling people what they should and shouldn't eat!" Lila followed Janet to the Unicorner.

"And me, too," Ellen said. "I've got to spend

every spare minute over the next few days reading *Tom Sawyer*, and it's all Elizabeth's fault." She, too, went off after Janet and Lila.

Aaron chuckled. "Elizabeth may be a Model Student, but she's not going to win any popularity contests," he said. He nodded in the direction of Bruce Patman, who was standing in the lunch line, talking to Mr. Edwards. "If you ask me, Bruce is a better candidate than Elizabeth any day."

As Aaron walked away, Jessica could feel her face flame red. What a horrible thing she had done, getting Elizabeth nominated as Model Student! It had completely and utterly changed her sister for the worse, and now everybody was mad at *her*, too. And if Elizabeth was this bad *before* she was named Model Student, what would she be like on Friday, *after* it was official?

Jessica swallowed hard and went to join Lila and Ellen at the Unicorner. It was too late to do anything about it now. The only way Elizabeth could be transformed back into her old self was for somebody *else* to be named Model Student. And *that* didn't seem very likely. Jessica's campaign had been much too successful.

*   *   *

Elizabeth had just left the cafeteria when she ran into Todd. "Hi, Todd," she said with a bright smile.

But Todd didn't smile back. "Something's really been bothering me," he said. "Winston told me that you gave him a hard time this morning about not paying attention in English class."

Elizabeth frowned. "I was just trying to be helpful," she said defensively. "After all, English isn't Winston's best subject. He admits that himself. It would be a lot better if he listened in class instead of goofing around."

"All you accomplished was to hurt Winston's feelings," Todd blurted out. "It's nobody's business but Winston's whether he pays attention in class or not."

For an instant Elizabeth was speechless. "I don't know what you mean," she said, careful to avoid meeting Todd's eyes.

"Sure you do," Todd said bluntly. "You're the one who wrote the essay on the importance of being an individual. Winston has the right to be himself, even if you don't agree with the way he's going about it."

"But Winston came to me for help," Elizabeth

protested. She was beginning to feel defensive. "He *asked* me."

"He asked you to help him with his *verbs*, Elizabeth," Todd replied calmly. "He didn't ask for a lesson in how to become a Model Student."

Elizabeth bit her lip and glanced down at her schedule. "I'm sorry," she said quickly, "but I can't talk any longer. It's time for me to check out some things for the *Sixers*."

"Yeah. Well, good-bye, Elizabeth." Todd gave her an odd smile before he turned and walked away.

That afternoon was one of the most uncomfortable Jessica had ever spent. In each of the afternoon classes she had with her twin, Elizabeth seemed determined to play the role of Responsible Class Citizen and to impress the teachers with her helpfulness.

After math class, Jessica was asking Ms. Wyler to explain the assignment again when Elizabeth came up to the desk. Ignoring Jessica, she charged right into the conversation.

"I've been thinking, Ms. Wyler, about the

decimal problems so many of the students are having trouble with," she said.

Ms. Wyler looked a little surprised at Elizabeth's interruption. "Oh?" she asked.

"Well, I think the students would learn much faster if you used more story problems. Story problems help people better understand an idea."

Jessica cringed. Her twin must have been reading the Model Student Guide again—the part where it said that a Model Student assisted teachers. Only this time, Elizabeth wasn't being helpful, she was being *critical*. Jessica had the sinking feeling that Ms. Wyler didn't like it one little bit.

Ms. Wyler frowned. "Do you really think more story problems are necessary?" she asked.

"Yes, I do." Elizabeth smiled nervously. "I'd be glad to make some up for you. I know how busy you are grading papers and everything."

Ms. Wyler's frown deepened, and Jessica braced herself for the teacher's reply. "I believe I can find a few minutes to make up some story problems—if and when it's necessary," she retorted.

*   *   *

Jessica was walking down the hall after the last class of the day when she bumped into Caroline Pearce.

"Have you heard the latest?" Caroline asked breathlessly. "There's a memo in Mr. Clark's office with *Bruce's* name on it!"

Jessica's heart rose hopefully. It seemed impossible, but maybe—just maybe—Bruce would be nominated instead of Elizabeth. If *that* happened, maybe Elizabeth would go back to being her old self! But then her heart sank. Bruce's name might be on a memo, but it was more likely to be a bad conduct report than a Model Student nomination.

Caroline hurried on to spread her news, and Amy, Julie, Maria, and Sophia joined Jessica. They all looked gloomy.

"Hi, you guys," Jessica said and sighed.

"Don't tell me," Amy said. "You're thinking about Elizabeth the Impossible."

"Did you hear what she said to Ms. Wyler?" Jessica asked.

"Let's face it. Elizabeth is on the road to ruin. The *Sixers* is falling apart because she insists on approving every little comma, her friends are getting fed up with her attitude, and pretty soon, even the *teachers* will be wondering if she's the Model Student they thought she was," Amy answered.

Sophia nodded. "In just a few days she's gotten nosier than Caroline Pearce."

"And bossier than Mrs. Arnette," Julie said. "She's got the biggest head I've ever seen."

Maria shook her head. "Maybe it's a new kind of fame disease."

"It's not *all* Elizabeth's fault," Amy proclaimed. "She *has* gone overboard on this Model Student thing. But it was *Pamela* who gave her the shove."

Sophia sighed. "With all that encouragement, no wonder Elizabeth thinks she's queen of the world."

"It's too bad Bruce isn't a serious candidate," Amy said regretfully. "If somebody else were named Model Student, maybe Elizabeth would stop acting like Miss Perfect and things would get back to normal."

The girls stopped talking as Brooke Dennis rushed to join them. "You'll never guess what I just heard," she said excitedly. "I came around the corner by the teachers' lounge, and I heard Ms. Wyler and Mr. Sweeney talking about nominating *Todd Wilkins* for the Model Student contest!"

"Todd!" Amy exclaimed. "Hey, now *there's* an idea!"

Jessica nodded thoughtfully. "Todd *would* be a good candidate," she said.

"Yeah," Brooke agreed. "He's a neat guy."

A scheme was beginning to form in Jessica's head, but she didn't like the scheme at all—it made her feel terribly disloyal to Elizabeth. She knew it would be much better—for Elizabeth and for everyone else—if Todd were chosen as Model Student. And *she* was the only one who could make it happen!

Eight

◇

Jessica was supposed to meet Mandy that afternoon after school, but there were a couple of important things she had to do first. She hurried to Ms. Wyler's classroom, where she found the math teacher grading papers.

"I never did get the assignment before," she explained to Ms. Wyler. "Elizabeth barged in and interrupted us."

Ms. Wyler smiled and picked up her lesson plan book. "Here it is, Jessica," she said. She read off the page numbers, and Jessica copied them into her notebook.

"Thanks," Jessica said as she put her notebook away. "I guess I could have gotten the assignment from Todd Wilkins. He's *such* a good student. He knows the answer to every problem, and he's *so* willing to help."

"Todd is a good student," Ms. Wyler agreed.

"A *model* student," Jessica replied emphatically. "He fits the description in the Model Student Guide better than anybody I know."

Ms. Wyler laughed. "Even better than Elizabeth?" she teased.

"Oh, sure," Jessica said. "The nice thing about Todd is that he never acts like he knows it all."

Ms. Wyler picked up her red pencil. "I think I'd better get on with my grading, Jessica. Good luck with the assignment."

Jessica left the room and met Mandy, who was waiting for her by the front door. "Where have you been?" Mandy asked impatiently. "I'd almost decided you weren't coming."

"It's a long story," Jessica sighed. "Are you sure you want to hear it?"

"Sure." Mandy looked at Jessica sympathetically. "It's about Elizabeth, isn't it? I heard that a lot of people are mad at her."

"Elizabeth wouldn't be in all this trouble

right now if it weren't for me," Jessica said regretfully.

"You?" Mandy asked.

"When I first heard about the Model Student competition," Jessica explained, "I went around to almost all the teachers and told them how terrific Elizabeth is and what a good Model Student she would make. And they all agreed. But now this Model Student stuff has gone to her head, and even her best friends think she's impossible. Anyway, I've decided it's time for me to undo what I did."

"How?" Mandy asked.

"Well, I've just talked to Ms. Wyler," Jessica replied. "I have the feeling teachers are going to nominate Todd instead of Elizabeth. But the trouble is that campaigning for Todd makes me feel really disloyal. Do you think I'm doing the right thing?"

"I don't know if it's right or not," Mandy replied truthfully. "You're doing what you think you *have* to do."

"What do you think?" she asked Mandy. "Should I tell Elizabeth that Todd might be nominated instead of her? Or should I let her find out through the grapevine at school tomorrow?"

"I'd tell her myself, if I were you," Mandy advised thoughtfully. "She may be acting like she's been crowned queen of the universe, but she's still your sister. You owe it to her."

Jessica nodded reluctantly. Mandy was right. But telling Elizabeth wasn't something she was looking forward to. Particularly since Todd's nomination was going to be her doing!

When Jessica got home, she made a sandwich and then went to look for Elizabeth. She found her in the den, folding a mountain of family laundry. It looked as if she had just washed every piece of linen the Wakefields owned.

"I thought I'd do the laundry so Mom wouldn't have to," Elizabeth said. Jessica noted that her sister was still wearing her Model Student uniform.

She decided to get straight to the point. "Brooke said she heard some of the teachers talking about nominating Todd for Model Student."

Elizabeth gave a short laugh. "I'm not surprised," she said. "The grapevine has been working overtime, and all kinds of ridiculous rumors are going around. I even heard that Bruce Patman is going to be nominated! Somebody claims to have seen his name on a memo in Mr. Clark's office. But of course, that's dumb." Elizabeth smirked. "Nobody in their right mind could imagine Bruce Patman as anything but Model Jerk."

"But Todd isn't at all like Bruce," Jessica said carefully, watching Elizabeth for her reaction. "People are saying he'd make a pretty good candidate."

Elizabeth finished folding a pillowcase. "Todd?" she repeated.

"He's got all the characteristics of a Model Student, don't you think?" Jessica continued. "I mean, he gets good grades, he's involved in a lot of different activities, and everybody respects him."

Elizabeth frowned and put her hands on her hips. "Whose side are you on, Jessica?" she demanded crossly. "Todd's or mine?" Then, without giving Jessica a chance to answer, she lifted her chin. "It just so happens that I *don't* agree that Todd Wilkins would be as good a candidate as I am. And it also happens that I'm right more often than *you* are."

Jessica stared open-mouthed at her twin. This was an Elizabeth she had never seen before.

"Well, I *am*," Elizabeth insisted, as if Jessica

had contradicted her. "Remember a few weeks ago, when you came up with the great idea of baby-sitting Chrissy Steele for a week? Our 'little sister' turned out to be a real disaster. And remember the time you decided to enter that stupid contest for the perfect French-oriented American family, and we all had to pretend to be French? Really, Jessica," she added scornfully, "you have to admit that your bright ideas are usually pretty dim-witted."

Jessica felt herself beginning to get angry, but she controlled herself. She wanted to reason with Elizabeth, not antagonize her. "I just think you should consider the possibility of—"

But Elizabeth interrupted her. "And then there was the time you decided that the Unicorns would print a newspaper of their own to compete with the *Sixers*! And the time you read Maria Slater's private notebook."

"Elizabeth," Jessica protested, "you really should stop and think—"

"And the time you got the weird idea that Steven's friend Chad Lucas liked you. And—"

"Elizabeth, you are being a total *jerk*!" Jessica shouted and stormed out of the den.

*   *   *

Even though Elizabeth felt smugly satisfied at having won the argument with Jessica, she didn't feel triumphant. She had to admit to herself that Todd was a very good candidate. In fact, in many ways he was a *better* candidate than she was. Not only was he a top student, but he was a star player on the basketball team *and* president of the debate club. And of course, he was a Scout, too, with lots of merit badges to his credit. Elizabeth frowned, thinking of the good-citizenship award he'd won for the clean-up campaign he'd organized last year. Yes, Todd Wilkins was a good candidate for Model Student. An *excellent* candidate.

Elizabeth sat down on the couch beside a stack of clean towels. When she thought of Todd as a candidate, a hard knot of jealousy tightened in her stomach. She realized that she wanted to be named Model Student more than she'd ever wanted anything before, and she didn't welcome competition from anyone—not even from Todd. But Elizabeth had never been a jealous person, and the way she was feeling bothered her. If she really liked Todd, she should wish him the very best, the same way he had wished *her* the best, shouldn't she?

Elizabeth was still puzzling over these questions when the phone rang. When she answered it, she discovered that it was a reporter from the Sweet Valley *Tribune*, and he wanted to speak to *her*!

"I'd like to write a short article about you, Elizabeth," the reporter said. "Because you're one of our Junior Journalists, your prize-winning *Teen Scene* essay is big news around the *Tribune*."

"That's great!" Elizabeth's spirits lifted. "When would you like to do it?"

"As soon as possible," the reporter replied. "My editor thought it would be a good idea if I interviewed you at school, so our photographer could get a picture of you with your friends. How about tomorrow during your lunch period? I could meet you by the cafeteria."

"That sounds fine," Elizabeth said. "I'll be looking forward to it." She put down the phone, and an excited smile spread across her face. She was going to be interviewed, and her picture would be in the *Tribune*! Everybody in Sweet Valley would hear about her prize-winning essay!

But as she went back to folding the laundry, Elizabeth thought again of Todd and her smile faded. How could she possibly be jealous of somebody she liked and admired as much as Todd?

Nine

◇

Elizabeth had just opened her locker on Tuesday morning when she looked up and saw Pamela making a beeline for her.

"Hi, Elizabeth," Pamela said happily. She glanced at Elizabeth's neat brown skirt and brown plaid blouse. "Hey, I like that outfit. Brown is one of your best colors." She noticed the lunch bag Elizabeth was putting into her locker. "I'm glad you brought your lunch today," she added. "I did, too. We're eating together, aren't we?"

"I have to do an interview at lunch," Elizabeth said, and she told Pamela about the phone call she'd received the night before from the *Trib-*

une reporter. "He's coming to do the interview today at noon, in the cafeteria. He said he wants to interview some of my friends, too. And he's bringing a photographer."

"An *interview*!" Pamela squealed. "Elizabeth, that's fabulous! Can I talk to the reporter? I'll tell him lots of wonderful things about you! Can I be in the picture, too?"

"If you want to," Elizabeth said a bit distractedly as she got her books out of her locker.

"Today is Tuesday," Pamela reminded her. "That means there are only four more days before you're officially named Model Student." She rubbed her hands together. "You'll be the most famous person in all of Sweet Valley! Maybe the *Tribune* will decide to do *another* story!"

"Um," Elizabeth said, not really listening to Pamela's excited chatter.

"You know what I heard this morning?" Pamela asked with a giggle. "I heard that Bruce Patman's name is on a memo in Mr. Clark's office. He thinks he's going to be nominated for Model Student. Isn't that a laugh?"

"Bruce isn't exactly the Model Student type," Elizabeth agreed as she shut her locker door.

"Yeah," Pamela said, "he's more the Model Arrogant type." She laughed, then glanced at Elizabeth to see if she thought her remark was funny, too.

But Elizabeth was in no mood for laughing. "Did you also hear that Todd Wilkins might be nominated?" she asked quietly.

"Todd Wilkins?" Pamela asked. Her face fell into a slight frown, then cleared. "Oh, *Todd*," she scoffed. "Don't worry, Elizabeth. Everybody knows that you're twice the candidate he is." She patted Elizabeth's shoulder. "You get better grades than he does, don't you?"

"Actually, we're about the same," Elizabeth said. "We're both on the honor roll."

"Well, you're the editor of the *Sixers*," Pamela pointed out. "That's a very important job."

"But Todd is president of the debate team," Elizabeth reminded her. "And he's a star player on the basketball team."

Pamela frowned. "But you were named Junior Journalist, and you won that *Teen Scene* contest. Remember?"

"Yes, but Todd got Sweet Valley's good citizenship award not very long ago for a clean-up campaign he organized," Elizabeth said.

"Hey, wait a minute," Pamela protested. "Whose side are you on? Yours or Todd's?"

"I'm just being realistic, that's all," Elizabeth replied. "If Todd is a better candidate, he deserves to get the nomination."

"But he's *not* better!" Pamela interrupted. "You're the best thing that's ever happened to Sweet Valley Middle School!" Pamela spoke loudly, and several kids gave her a curious look as they walked past.

Elizabeth was embarrassed by Pamela's enthusiasm and wished she hadn't spoken quite so loudly. "I don't want to kid myself into believing I'm something I'm not."

"You're in no danger of that," Pam said firmly. "Take my advice and forget all about Todd Wilkins. He's not going to win this nomination. You are."

For the rest of that morning, whenever Elizabeth approached a group, they'd suddenly stopped talking. Elizabeth had the feeling that they had been talking about Todd. She also noticed that lots of kids were hanging around with him, laughing and talking and having a good time. What made this all the more noticeable was the fact that nobody was hanging around with *her*. In fact, with the exception of Pamela, who followed her faithfully from one class to another, nobody said anything more than "Hi, Elizabeth," to her. She couldn't even find Amy, Sophia or Julie, to ask them if they wanted to be interviewed with her. Somehow they seemed to disappear after every class.

"I can't figure it out," Elizabeth told Pamela after gym class. "Why is everybody giving me the cold shoulder? I feel like I've been deserted by all my friends."

Pamela laughed lightly. "You're imagining things, Elizabeth," she said. "People aren't giving you the cold shoulder. *I'm* here, aren't I?"

"Yes, but you're my—" Elizabeth stopped herself. She had been about to say *best friend*. Amy had always been her best friend. But where was Amy? And Sophia and Julie and Brooke? And Jessica? She had been avoiding her ever since Elizabeth had told her family about the interview last night at dinner. Suddenly, Elizabeth felt terribly alone.

"Don't worry about it, Elizabeth," Pamela said reassuringly as she put an arm around her shoulders. "People are just jealous, that's all.

Wait until lunchtime, when they see you being interviewed by that *Tribune* reporter and having your picture taken. That'll bring them flocking around.''

Elizabeth shook her head. What Pamela said didn't fit with what she knew about her friends. Amy wasn't the jealous type, and neither were Sophia and Julie. She was glad when she got to social studies class and could sit down by herself and hide behind her book. She had some thinking to do, and she couldn't do it with Pamela rattling on every minute about how wonderful she was.

By the time social studies class was over, Elizabeth had decided that she had to talk to Todd. After all, he *was* her boyfriend. Their last conversation hadn't been so great, but that had been an exception. A few minutes with Todd would make her feel better about everything.

She caught up with Todd just before lunch hour. He was standing beside the drinking fountain.

"Hello, Elizabeth," Todd said. He bent over and took a long drink from the water fountain.

Elizabeth cleared her throat. "I—I just want to congratulate you," she said to the back of his head. "I—I heard that you may be nominated as Model Student."

Todd straightened up. "Thanks, Elizabeth," he said as he wiped his mouth. "Yeah, that's what I heard, too." He looked at her carefully. "But you know what they say about the grapevine. Half of what you hear through it isn't true."

"I know." Elizabeth laughed. "Like that story about Bruce Patman's name being on a memo in Mr. Clark's office. That was pretty funny."

Todd nodded. "Yeah, right. It's even funnier when you know the truth. That memo was a detention slip."

"I thought it might be something like that," Elizabeth said. "That *is* funny."

"I heard something that isn't funny at all," Todd said. "Something about the way you've been treating your friends. What's gotten into you lately, Elizabeth? You're impossible. The girl I used to like would never say anything to hurt anyone's feelings."

Elizabeth looked up at him, a cold feeling at the pit of her stomach. The girl he *used* to like? Did that mean that Todd did not consider himself her boyfriend anymore?

"Elizabeth!" Elizabeth was vaguely aware that

Pamela was tugging at her arm. "It's time for you to meet the reporter from the *Tribune*! You know—for your interview and the photography session! Have you forgotten?"

Todd's lips curled into a smile. "Go on, Elizabeth," he said. "Sounds like your coach doesn't want you to be late for your big performance."

"But, Todd—" Elizabeth began.

Todd's smile faded and he shook his head. "Go on. It's time for the Model Student to meet the press."

With a heavy heart, Elizabeth turned away and walked quickly down the hall. Pamela jogged along beside her.

"What were you talking to Todd about?" Pamela asked breathlessly. "I certainly hope you weren't congratulating him. I'd hate for anybody to think you were throwing in the towel."

Elizabeth suddenly stopped and faced Pamela. She felt a sour taste in her mouth. Why was Pamela always interfering with her friends? She stared at Pamela for a moment and then, without a word, she turned and walked away.

"Wait, Elizabeth!" Pamela cried, waving her lunch bag. "Don't you want me to be there when you meet the reporter and the photographer? I can help you think of things to say, and—"

"I'd rather handle this myself, thank you," Elizabeth said over her shoulder as she kept on walking.

Elizabeth had been looking forward to her big interview with the *Tribune* reporter. But after what just happened with Todd and Pamela, she was feeling terribly unsure of herself, and she was certainly in no mood to talk about her achievements. Still, the reporter was expecting her, and she knew there was no way she could get out of it.

Elizabeth met the reporter and the photographer at the door to the cafeteria. She was aware that the other kids were watching her curiously. After the introductions, the reporter looked around the cafeteria.

"Where are your friends?" he asked. "And where's your twin? I wanted to include her in the interview."

Elizabeth couldn't see Jessica anywhere. She knew Jessica must be totally fed up with her. Why else would she deliberately miss a chance of getting her name in the local paper? Elizabeth continued to scan the room and finally spotted Amy,

Sophia, and Julie sitting at their favorite table in the back of the cafeteria. After the way they had been avoiding her, she thought they would probably not want to be a part of the interview. "Um, I was thinking we could do the interview by ourselves," she suggested.

The reporter shook his head. "Nope. My editor wants me to be sure and get your friends' reaction to your winning the contest," he said. "It's all part of the story."

Hesitantly, Elizabeth led the reporter and the photographer over toward Amy, Sophia, and Julie's table.

"An interview?" Amy said. She glanced at Julie and Sophia, and they both nodded. "Sure." Amy shrugged. "Why not?" Elizabeth hoped that the reporter didn't notice that Amy's tone was cool and that the looks the others gave her weren't the friendliest.

For the rest of the lunch hour, Elizabeth sat with Amy, Julie, and Sophia and answered the reporter's questions, feeling more and more awful every minute. He asked about the *Teen Scene* essay, and then he asked about the Model Student competition. During the interview, the photographer was snapping pictures, and the kids at the other tables were watching and listening curiously.

Finally, the reporter flipped to a clean page in his notebook. "One last question," he said, turning to Amy. "How does it feel to have a friend who wins prizes and awards and gets her picture in the paper?"

Amy glanced at Elizabeth, then down at her lunch. "I guess it depends on the friend," she said slowly. "If she's the kind of person who doesn't get a big head, it's a lot of fun. But if she's the kind of person who begins to think she's queen or something, that's *no* fun. Pretty soon, she won't have any friends left, except for the ones who flatter her all the time."

Elizabeth pulled in her breath. She felt as if she'd been socked in the stomach. Did Amy think she had a big head? She glanced at Julie and Sophia. What did they think? But they refused to meet her eyes, and she couldn't tell what was going on in their heads.

The reporter put away his pencil. "And which type is Elizabeth? Off the record, of course," he added jokingly.

Elizabeth held her breath. Amy shrugged. "Time will tell," she said noncommittally.

The reporter stood up and grinned. "Well, I guess that's it, girls," he said. "I think we've got a super story here. Thanks for your help." He looked at Elizabeth. "Can you tell me how to get to the parking lot entrance, Elizabeth? We came the long way around, and I'm lost."

"Sure," Elizabeth said quickly and stood up. She couldn't sit there and face Amy, Julie, and Sophia and wonder what they were thinking about her. And she certainly didn't want to ask them.

Elizabeth had not been able to find Jessica during lunch because Jessica had decided not to go. At first, she had struggled with her decision. After all, a chance to get her name in the newspaper, even as the twin sister of an impossible perfectionist, was not to be easily dismissed. But finally, Jessica decided that getting the old Elizabeth back was much more important than seeing her own name in print.

So she spent the hour dropping in on her teachers. She went to one after another, casually mentioning that she thought Todd would be a great Model Student, or that Elizabeth thought that Todd was the best candidate, or that their friends couldn't imagine a more perfect Model Student than Todd. One after another, the teachers agreed with her, and not one seemed surprised that she had brought up the subject. She even spoke to Coach Cassells, the basketball coach.

The coach nodded when Jessica said that a lot of kids were talking about Todd and hoping he'd be nominated.

"I've been thinking about Todd, too," he said. "He's a great kid."

Jessica smiled. "Do you think he'll be nominated?" she asked eagerly.

Coach Cassells's eyes twinkled. "You never know," he said. "But his chances are better than some I could name."

As Jessica was turning the corner after leaving Coach Cassells, she found Pamela McDonald waiting for her, hands on her hips.

"Jessica Wakefield," Pamela exclaimed. "You should be ashamed. You've betrayed your sister!"

"What gave you the right to listen in on my conversation?" Jessica demanded angrily.

"I'm Elizabeth's best friend," Pamela said,

lifting her chin. "That's what gave me the right! What's she going to say when I tell her that her twin sister is campaigning for the enemy?"

Jessica paled. "You're not going to tell her!"

Pamela gave her a self-righteous look. "Of course I am," she replied. "Elizabeth has the right to know that her own sister is stacking the deck against her." Pamela turned and stalked away, leaving Jessica staring after her open-mouthed.

After Elizabeth had shown the reporter and the photographer out to the parking lot, she thought of some work she could do on the *Sixers* that would keep her from having to face Amy and the others. It might also keep her from thinking about other things that had happened that morning, particularly what Todd had said and how Pamela had acted.

Elizabeth headed for Mr. Bowman's room. But when she turned the handle, the door was locked, and once again she could hear voices coming from inside the room. One voice she recognized as Mr. Bowman's, and this time, she recognized the other voice as belonging to Mr. Clark. Elizabeth couldn't make out much of what was being said, but she did hear one word. *Wil-*

kins. Mr. Bowman and Mr. Clark were talking about Todd! They had to be discussing whether he should be nominated for Model Student!

For a second, Elizabeth hesitated. The conversation that was going on in Mr. Bowman's room was private. But she just *had* to know whether or not Todd was serious competition!

Trembling, Elizabeth moved closer to the door. She couldn't hear anything very clearly. Even though she was almost touching the door, the voices were nothing more than a fuzzy mumble. The only other thing she heard was *Wakefield*. She just *had* to know what they were saying!

Holding her breath, Elizabeth leaned over and pressed her ear against the frosted glass window in the door. But to her dismay, the voices seemed quieter. She closed her eyes, leaned her ear against the door as hard as she could, and tried to concentrate.

And then, suddenly, the door opened. Elizabeth tried to catch herself as she almost fell into the room, but she felt a strong hand pushing her back up. And then she heard Mr. Clark's voice.

"Elizabeth Wakefield! You've been eavesdropping!"

Ten

◇

For a moment, Elizabeth just stood there, her face flaming. She felt like crying, but she couldn't make a sound.

"I don't believe it," Mr. Bowman said. He shook his head helplessly and looked at Mr. Clark. "I never thought Elizabeth would eavesdrop on a private conversation."

"Neither did I." Mr. Clark fastened stern eyes on Elizabeth. "Young lady, I will see you in my office in ten minutes. Go on and wait for me."

Without a word, Elizabeth left the room and walked down the hall to Mr. Clark's office, where she sat down to wait. It was the longest ten minutes of her life. While she was waiting, she thought of all the things that had happened since the morning Mr. Davis had first told them about the Model Student competition. She thought about how she had found out that Mr. Bowman wanted to nominate her. She thought about how she'd gone out of her way to look and dress and act the part of the Model Student. She remembered the new rule she'd laid down to the *Sixers* staff, and Patrick's question: *"Who does she think she is, Queen Elizabeth?"* Her face grew red as she recalled the way she'd tried to talk Jessica into playing the harp and going for a six o'clock jog. And then how she'd tossed out her dad's coffee and Steven's junk food. How could she have been such a dictator!

Miserably, Elizabeth squeezed her eyes shut and balled her hands into tight fists. All those tyrannical things she had done were bad enough, but they weren't half as bad as the hurtful things she had said to her friends—and all because she had wanted to make herself look caring and superresponsible!

Mr. Clark came through the door. "You may come into my office now," he said. A moment later, he handed her a week's worth of detention slips and a note to her parents. According to the detention slips, she was to report to the principal's office every day after school for a week. "I think you'd better read the note," he told her.

Elizabeth bit her lip and read the note. "Elizabeth Wakefield has been required to serve five days' detention because she was caught eavesdropping on a teachers' conversation."

"I want you to take that note home and get your parents' signature on it," Mr. Clark said in a kind but firm voice. "Bring it back to me tomorrow."

"Yes, sir," Elizabeth whispered.

Mr. Clark cleared his throat. "I'm very sorry this happened, Elizabeth. I always believed that you were a trustworthy person." He didn't mention the Model Student competition, but he didn't have to. Elizabeth could repeat from memory the Model Student Guide. *A Model Student is trustworthy.* Now that Mr. Clark knew she couldn't be trusted, her chances for getting the nomination were completely gone.

Elizabeth left Mr. Clark's office and walked slowly down the crowded hall. There were kids all around her, but she was so deep in thought that she didn't even notice them. She knew where she had gone wrong. She had let her desire to win the Model Student competition take charge of her life. She had become a dictator who tried to make all her friends, and even her sister, into carbon copies of the Model Student *she* wanted to be. She had forgotten that everybody had the right to be an individual, even if that meant being lazy or daydreaming in class. And she'd forgotten something she had learned a long time ago: that *friends* were the most important things a person could have, more important than prizes or awards or fancy titles.

Elizabeth quickened her step. She might have destroyed her chances at becoming a Model Student. But that didn't mean she'd *completely* destroyed her friendships, too. She could still apologize to Winston and Janet. She could patch things up with Amy, Sophia, and Julie. She could take away that stupid rule she had made for the *Sixers* and tell Patrick and Nora she'd been wrong. And when she had done all that, she could tell Todd that she had gone back to being the Elizabeth he knew and liked.

The bell for the next class was ringing by the

time Elizabeth got to her locker to get her books. Pamela was standing there waiting.

"I have to talk to you, Elizabeth," she said urgently. "There's something you should know."

Elizabeth drew in a deep breath. She never wanted to hear another word of Pamela's flattery. "I don't want to hear it, Pamela," she said quietly. "Now, excuse me, but I don't want to be late to class."

"But you have to hear this," Pamela cried as she grabbed Elizabeth's arm. "Just a little while ago, I heard Jessica telling Coach Cassels that *Todd* was the best candidate for Model Student. Your very own twin has *betrayed* you!"

Elizabeth beamed. "She has? That's wonderful! Todd deserves the nomination more than anybody I know."

Pamela's mouth fell open. "But Elizabeth!" she wailed. "Jessica's spoiling your chances! You're *twice* the Model Student Todd Wilkins is!"

"Pamela," Elizabeth said firmly, "that's enough. I don't want to hear any more about how great I am. And as far as being Model Student is concerned, I blew my chance. Mr. Clark caught me eavesdropping at Mr. Bowman's door, and he gave me a week's detention."

Pamela's eyes grew big. "*You* got a week's detention?" she whispered.

"And I think it would be good for both of us," Elizabeth said more gently, "if we didn't spend a lot of time together anymore."

Pamela's shoulders slumped. "Maybe you're right," she said. "A week's detention!" she muttered as she walked away.

Jessica had planned to go shopping with the Unicorns that afternoon after school. But after what had happened with Pamela, she told Lila that something very important had come up. She had decided to confess to Elizabeth exactly what she had done and why—*before* Pamela McDonald spilled the beans. When the last bell rang, she ran straight for Elizabeth's locker.

"Elizabeth," Jessica said when she reached her sister, "I need to talk to you. It's crucial."

"I know," Elizabeth said calmly as she put some books on the top shelf of her locker. "I need to talk to you, too, but I have to do detention first."

Jessica stared at her twin in amazement.

"Detention!" she gasped. "*You're* doing detention? What *for*?"

"It's a long story." Elizabeth sighed, but there was a twinkle in her eye. "I'll tell you later, OK?"

"Sure," Jessica said. "I'll wait." She shook her head. What had Elizabeth done to get detention?

A half-hour later, Jessica met Elizabeth outside of Mr. Clark's office. "Listen, Jessica," Elizabeth said, "before you tell me whatever it is you have to tell me, I want to thank you."

"Thank me for what?" Jessica asked as they left the school building.

"For telling Coach Cassels that Todd is the best candidate for Model Student," Elizabeth said. "Pamela told me all about it."

Jessica's mouth dropped open. She couldn't believe her ears. "You're thanking me for *that*?" she managed to say at last. "You mean, you're not mad?" Jessica swallowed. "Would you thank me if I told you that I've also talked to the other teachers to try to get *them* to nominate Todd?"

"If you hadn't done it already, I'd have to," Elizabeth replied. "Todd *is* the best candidate." Elizabeth told Jessica the whole story of her getting the detention. "I know I don't deserve to be Sweet Valley Middle School's Model Student. Anyway, I'd rather people think of me as their *friend*, not as their model." She shook her head. "I'll bet everyone got pretty sick of me giving them lessons on how to be perfect!"

Jessica threw her arms around her sister. "Is it really true?" she squealed happily. "Has the old Elizabeth come back for good?"

"I certainly hope so!" Elizabeth giggled. "To tell you the truth, it was getting pretty tiring trying to be a saint all the time—especially when I know down deep that I'm *not* one!"

For the next few days, Elizabeth was very busy. Serving detention took up a half-hour every afternoon, and then she had to go straight home because her parents had grounded her for the week. It had been terribly embarrassing, explaining to them why she'd gotten detention. She knew that they were disappointed in her.

Elizabeth was busy with apologies, too. She started with Winston, and then she went on to all the other kids she had offended over the past week. It wasn't easy, especially when it came to people like Janet and Lila, but Elizabeth did her best and the list of people she had to apologize to got shorter and shorter.

And being so busy meant that she had no time to do some of the other things she had gotten into the habit of doing. She had no time to lecture anybody about paying attention in class or about taking up enriching hobbies. She had no time to approve the *Sixers* articles, so she told the staff that she was canceling the new rule. And she certainly had no time to set the table when it was not her turn!

But she *did* have time to talk to Todd. On Thursday, the day before the special assembly at which the name of the Model Student candidate would be announced, she stopped by his locker. It had taken her two full days to work up the courage to talk to him.

"Hi, Todd," she said.

"Hi, Elizabeth," Todd said warmly. "How are things?"

Elizabeth grinned at Todd. "Things are just fine—now," she said. "But I've been really busy trying to make up for my behavior in the last week."

Todd nodded. "Yeah, I heard," he said. "Winston told me you apologized to him." Todd touched her arm. "It's nice to have you back, Elizabeth."

Elizabeth felt a warm glow. "It's nice to *be* back," she said.

"Want to sit together at the assembly tomorrow?" Todd asked as he closed his locker.

"Sure! See you there," she said. As she walked away she felt warm and happy inside. She was hoping that tomorrow she would get to see Todd chosen as Sweet Valley Middle School's Model Student.

The next morning, Elizabeth and Jessica met Todd outside the assembly hall, and the three of them walked in together. They found seats in the second row and waited for Mr. Clark to begin.

Finally, after the teachers had taken seats on the stage, Mr. Clark got up and went to the podium. After a few announcements and some introductory remarks, he said, "And now I'll get down to the business we've all been waiting for—the announcement of Sweet Valley Middle School's Model Stdent. As you know, each school is permitted to name at least one Model

Student. Because of its size, however, Sweet Valley Middle School is permitted to name two."

There was a stir as students shifted in their seats, and Elizabeth and Jessica traded glances. *Two* Model Students! That was an idea that had never occurred to either of them.

"Maybe Bruce Patman is going to get it after all," Jessica said with a giggle, and Elizabeth grinned.

"So I have two names to announce," Mr. Clark was saying. "The first one is Todd Wilkins."

Todd looked happily at Elizabeth as he stood and went up to the stage. Everybody applauded, but Elizabeth clapped loudest of all. She'd been right. Todd *was* the best qualified person. But who was the other Model Student?

"And our second Model Student," Mr. Clark said, "is—Elizabeth Wakefield!"

"Me?" Elizabeth gasped. "Impossible!"

Elizabeth stood up. The applause sounded like thunder in her ears. It was just like in her dream, except that Todd was sharing the spotlight with her.

"Congratulations, Elizabeth!" Todd said when the assembly was over and they were heading back to class. He leaned over and kissed her on the cheek.

"Congratulations, Todd." Elizabeth beamed back at him.

"Congratulations, you two!" Jessica cried, hugging both of them.

"Terrific, you guys!" Winston cried. "I can't think of a better team! Rah, rah! Let's hear it for Elizabeth and Todd!"

"Elizabeth and Todd!" their friends cheered, following Winston's lead. And for the next few minutes, Elizabeth and Todd were surrounded by their very own cheering squad. Elizabeth couldn't remember when she had ever been so happy.

On Saturday morning, Jessica and the rest of the members of the Boosters, Sweet Valley Middle School's cheering squad, were gathered at Lila's house for what was supposed to be a meeting and an extra practice session.

"Come on, you guys," Amy said, placing her hands on her hips and glaring at her fellow Boosters, who were lazing around the well-furnished room. "We *said* this was going to be a cheering practice."

"Yeah," Grace Oliver added. "And a meeting

on whether or not we should try any new cheers at the big Middle School Championships coming up."

"Relax, will you?" Lila said. She lifted her head from the couch on which she was stretched out and looked at Amy and Grace with amusement. "We have plenty of time to talk about new uniforms and plenty of time to practice. Besides, we're already a fabulous squad. I really don't see why we have to have this extra practice. I mean, it *is* Saturday morning!"

Jessica kept her eyes on the TV as she spoke. "Lila's right, Amy. Saturday mornings are for hanging around and doing nothing. And after what I've just been through with Elizabeth, I can use all the relaxation I can get."

Grace shrugged and plopped down onto the floor by the couch. "Fine with me. If you guys don't care about the Championships, then neither do I."

"Well *I* do," Amy announced. "Face it, you guys. We stink. We're pathetic. And we're going to make fools of ourselves at the Championships if we don't get in some serious practice."

"Yeah." Grace giggled. "Amy's right. Even Winston Egbert is a better cheerleader than we are. Remember when he led that cheer for Elizabeth and Todd yesterday after the assembly?''

Jessica turned away from the TV and looked curiously at Grace. "That's the second time you've mentioned Winston Egbert in a week. First you told me you thought he might make a good Model Student. And now you say he's a better cheerleader than we are. What's going on, anyway?''

Lila laughed. "Grace acts like she's Winston's personal agent. If I didn't know better, I'd say she *likes* Winston.''

Amy picked up her baton and twirled it over her head. "All right. If you guys want to spend the entire morning making fun of Winston—someone who has absolutely nothing to do with the Boosters and who never will have anything to do with the Boosters—that's fine with me. *I'm* going to practice. I, for one, don't want to be the laughingstock of the Championships.''

Grace got up from her place by the couch. "Yeah, let's leave Winston out of it," she said. "Amy's right. Winston's got nothing to do with the Boosters. But Sweet Valley Middle School does. It's hosting the Championships. We owe it to our school to be the most fabulous we can be. Right?''

Jessica pressed the off button on the remote control and sighed dramatically. "OK, OK. But you'd better watch it," she said, looking at Amy and Grace, who were shoving aside a table to make room for their cheers. "You two are beginning to sound like Model Students. And I, for one, have had about all the perfection I can take!''

Tamara tossed aside the fashion magazine she had been reading and stood up to help Amy and Grace. "And I've had about all I can take of Bruce Patman lately. He's been more obnoxious than ever! Did you hear how he lied about being nominated for Model Student? Please!''

Lila groaned as she swung her legs off the coach. "*All* boys are obnoxious, if you ask me. Even the cute ones. I'm glad the Unicorn Club is exclusive in more ways than one. Can you imagine boys in the club? How could we ever have any fun?''

"And what about the Boosters?" Janet asked. "You know, some middle school cheering squads have boys *and* girls on them. Can you imagine?''

A sound of disgust rose from the girls, except Amy. "I don't know, you guys. The more I think about it, the more sense it seems to make to allow boys onto the squad. We'd be able to do more exciting stunts."

Janet folded her arms and stared at the girls in the room. "If *I* have anything to say about it, there will never, ever be a boy admitted to the Unicorns *or* to the Boosters. And that's the final word!"

Will the Boosters allow a boy to join their squad? Find out in Sweet Valley Twins #52, **BOOSTER BOYCOTT.**

The most exciting story ever in Sweet Valley history—

COMING IN JULY 1991

FRANCINE PASCAL'S

SWEET VALLEY Saga

THE **WAKEFIELDS** OF **SWEET VALLEY**

THE SWEET VALLEY SAGA tells the incredible story of the lives and times of five generations of brave and beautiful young women who were Jessica and Elizabeth's ancestors. Their story is the story of America: from the danger of the pioneering days to the glamour of the roaring twenties, the sacrifice and romance of World War II to the rebelliousness of the Sixties, right up to the present-day Sweet Valley. A dazzling novel of unforgettable lives and love both lost and won, THE SWEET VALLEY SAGA is Francine Pascal's most memorable, exciting, and wonderful Sweet Valley book ever.

Be The First to Read It!

AN-251 6/91

SWEET VALLEY TWINS™

Join Jessica and Elizabeth for
big adventure in exciting
SWEET VALLEY TWINS SUPER EDITIONS
and **SWEET VALLEY TWINS CHILLERS.**

☐ **#1: CLASS TRIP**   15588-1/$2.95

☐ **#2: HOLIDAY MISCHIEF**   15641-1/$2.95

☐ **#3: THE BIG CAMP SECRET**   15707-8/$2.95

☐ **SWEET VALLEY TWINS SUPER SUMMER
FUN BOOK by Laurie Pascal Wenk**
                   15816-3/$3.50/3.95

Elizabeth shares her favorite summer projects &
Jessica gives you pointers on parties. Plus:
fashion tips, space to record your favorite
summer activities, quizzes, puzzles, a summer
calendar, photo album, scrapbook, address book
& more!

CHILLERS

☐ **#1: THE CHRISTMAS GHOST**   15767-1/$3.50

☐ **#2: THE GHOST IN THE GRAVEYARD**
                   15801-5/$3.50

☐ **#3: THE CARNIVAL GHOST**   15859-7/$2.95

Bantam Books, Dept. SVT6, 414 East Golf Road, Des Plaines, IL 60016

Please send me the items I have checked above. I am enclosing $_____
(please add $2.50 to cover postage and handling). Send check or money
order, no cash or C.O.D.s please.

Mr/Ms _____

Address _____

City/State _____ Zip _____

                                                SVT6-7/91

Please allow four to six weeks for delivery.
Prices and availability subject to change without notice.

SWEET VALLEY TWINS ™

☐	15681-0	**TEAMWORK #27**	$2.75
☐	15688-8	**APRIL FOOL! #28**	$2.75
☐	15695-0	**JESSICA AND THE BRAT ATTACK #29**	$2.75
☐	15715-9	**PRINCESS ELIZABETH #30**	$2.95
☐	15727-2	**JESSICA'S BAD IDEA #31**	$2.75
☐	15747-7	**JESSICA ON STAGE #32**	$2.99
☐	15753-1	**ELIZABETH'S NEW HERO #33**	$2.99
☐	15766-3	**JESSICA, THE ROCK STAR #34**	$2.99
☐	15772-8	**AMY'S PEN PAL #35**	$2.95
☐	15778-7	**MARY IS MISSING #36**	$2.99
☐	15779-5	**THE WAR BETWEEN THE TWINS #37**	$2.99
☐	15789-2	**LOIS STRIKES BACK #38**	$2.99
☐	15798-1	**JESSICA AND THE MONEY MIX-UP #39**	$2.95
☐	15806-6	**DANNY MEANS TROUBLE #40**	$2.99
☐	15810-4	**THE TWINS GET CAUGHT #41**	$2.95
☐	15824-4	**JESSICA'S SECRET #42**	$2.95
☐	15835-X	**ELIZABETH'S FIRST KISS #43**	$2.95
☐	15837-6	**AMY MOVES IN #44**	$2.95
☐	15843-0	**LUCY TAKES THE REINS #45**	$2.95
☐	15849-X	**MADEMOISELLE JESSICA #46**	$2.95

Bantam Books, Dept. SVT5, 414 East Golf Road, Des Plaines, IL 60016

Please send me the items I have checked above. I am enclosing $_____ (please add $2.50 to cover postage and handling). Send check or money order, no cash or C.O.D.s please.

Mr/Ms _____

Address _____

City/State _____ Zip _____

SVT5-7/91

Please allow four to six weeks for delivery.
Prices and availability subject to change without notice.